MISTAKE OF MAGIC

REVERSE HAREM FANTASY

POWER OF FIVE BOOK 2

BY ALEX LIDELL

DANGER BEARING PRESS

ALEX LIDELL

MISTAKE OF MAGIC

POWER OF FIVE BOOK 2

New Adult Fantasy Romance

POWER OF FIVE (Reverse Harem Fantasy)

POWER OF FIVE

MISTAKE OF MAGIC

TRIAL OF THREE

Young Adult Fantasy Novels

TIDES

FIRST COMMAND (Prequel Novella)

AIR AND ASH

WAR AND WIND

SEA AND SAND

SCOUT

TRACING SHADOWS

UNRAVELING DARKNESS

TILDOR

THE CADET OF TILDOR

~

SIGN UP FOR NEW RELEASE NOTIFICATIONS at
www.subscribepage.com/TIDES

LERA

I circle, my hands raised, my breath coming hard. Rapid. Nothing like the calm male before me, whose every movement is water incarnate. Beads of sweat snake down my skin, stinging my eyes and salting my lips. A distant part of my mind remembers this mountain path being bitingly cold, but that was an eternity ago, when my lungs had all the air they wanted.

The soft crack of twigs beneath my leather boots mocks me gently. The male's feet make no sound, as if the drying autumn leaves have no power to get in his way.

Bending my knees, I launch forward, bracing for the impact. I aim my shoulder for the male's thigh, my hands ready to chop his knees just as soon as I lock against his body. No hesitation, that's the key. Move through him. Penetrate. Now that I'm committed, one of us will be hitting the ground. Him or me.

It will hurt a lot less if it's him.

My shoulder strikes a wall of deadly, immortal flesh. *Penetrate. Penetrate. Penetrate.* I keep moving, shoving, as if my true target isn't the male himself but something beyond him. The male's musky, metallic scent fills my nose. My legs strain with the burn of depleted muscle. The wall that is him holds. One heartbeat. Two. On the third, it finally wavers, then gives.

The male lands gracefully on his back, my body sprawled a great deal less gracefully atop him. My sweat-slicked cheek slides across the hard squares of his bare abdomen. And I realize I was very wrong: It hurts just as much to land on top of the male as on the ground, his coiled muscles offering all the cushioning of bloody rocks.

Before I can gather myself, I realize I'm still moving. *We* are still moving.

The male's muscled arms wrap around me, his hips continuing the motion that I kindled. I feel myself pressed against him as he rolls fluidly over his shoulder, reversing our positions. It's my back on the ground now, the twigs digging into my flesh while the male straddles my body, his hands pinning my wrists to the dirt. His face floats above mine, piercing blue eyes lit with frustration. His sharply carved jaw is clenched even tighter than usual, and a wisp of blond hair that's escaped his bun drops down to tickle my cheek.

"Mortal." His voice is a low velvet that vibrates through my body.

"You are a bastard, Coal," I say through clenched teeth.

Coal raises a brow. His hips shift, somehow making him feel three times heavier. He lowers his face to mine, the hair's distance between us saturated with his body's blazing heat. His eyes meet mine, the purple tinge around his irises hidden. "You stopped paying attention the instant your takedown succeeded."

I wonder whether that purple is a trick of the light or a reflection of Coal's thoughts. It would be very interesting if it were the latter, though I doubt it's possible.

"Mortal." Coal squeezes my wrists harder to get my attention, his voice dangerously quiet. "Next time your mind goes on holiday, I'll crack a rib or two."

"Empty . . . threat." I fight to get the words past the pressure on my chest.

Coal's sharp canines bare themselves. "Shall we wager on it? Shade can heal you afterward, but I promise it won't feel good."

Shit. My stomach clenches, a rush of unease pushing my heart into a gallop and my attention on Coal to razor-sharp focus. I trust the warrior with my life, not with my enjoyment of it. He just might crack ribs if that brutal mind of his thought it a good idea.

Coal slides off me, extending a hand to pull me to my feet.

I climb up slowly, stretching out the moment in hopes of finding my suddenly elusive balance, of convincing my heart to slow. Just when I think I've cracked through Coal's facade, I discover a new level of steel underneath.

I straighten my shirt, brush dirt and leaves off the back of my head. I'm wearing what has become my customary

3

training outfit: supple black leather pants, soft boots that lace up the back of my calves, and a fitted linen shirt. I learned my lesson about wearing loose clothes a week ago—when Coal proved he wasn't above yanking me around with extra fabric.

Coal presses his hand between my shoulder blades, nudging a finger beneath my auburn braid. "You are all right. Feel the solid ground beneath your feet, and breathe."

And here I thought myself better at hiding emotions.

"I can smell fear," Coal says, as if having heard my thoughts. For a male who thinks a cracked rib to be an acceptable teaching aid, his awareness of my body is frighteningly perceptive. Switching his grip to my shoulders, Coal twists me about to face him. Sweat drips lazily down the deep groove between his pectorals, and I have to force myself not to track it with my eyes. Like all of my males, Coal is large for an immortal fae warrior, and I—being small even for a human—barely reach his corded shoulder. Coal's face tips down, clear blue eyes studying mine. "I can smell the absence of it too, mortal. And when you stop being a little bit afraid of the consequences, you forget that you are training to defend yourself against the darkness of Mors."

"I think you are confusing 'a little bit afraid' and 'paralyzingly terrified.'" I step closer to him, reaching for his body with one hand.

Coal's arms stiffen. "I don't hug, mortal."

"Says the male who was just sitting half-naked atop my chest."

"I do as much to River, Shade, and Tye. If it makes you

feel better, I do not hug any of them afterward either." Coal releases my shoulders and steps back, reclaiming the all-too-familiar distance between us. The same distance he keeps between himself and everyone. If I didn't know better, I'd say that this male—the one who took half a dozen arrows in silence to protect my life—was afraid.

Perhaps I don't know better. Slavery in the dark realm of Mors could have left scars beyond those on his wrists and flesh.

"Get some breakfast," Coal calls, turning in the opposite direction of camp. "I'm going to wash up."

I watch him walk away. "The lake is freezing," I call, but he only lifts a dismissive hand in response. His black pants cling to his hips, which flare into a broad back, crisscrossed with latent muscle and jagged scars. That mysterious tattoo twists down his spine, practically begging my fingers to explore it.

Shaking my head, I start through the dense autumn wood toward the scent of frying meat. After a week of trekking through the neutral lands—skirting along the base of the mountain range that dominated our horizon in Slait Court, and then rising into it, through whispering green foothills and forests ringing with birdsong—the fae and I are now only four hours from the Citadel. Perched atop the summit of a forested mountain, the Citadel is a court unto itself, complete with a strategic view of its territory.

Four hours and then we'll be there. Asking the Elders Council to accept our oath as a quint. My chest tightens, nausea shifting my stomach. If the rest of the Elders Council is anything like Klarissa—the gorgeous,

5

manipulative viper who tried to have me killed—then the five of us are walking into a predator's open maw. Not that the males have been anything but cavalier about it, their quiet discussion focused primarily on how to continue killing dark things coming out of Mors without those dark things killing me in the process.

As for Klarissa, River said he'll handle her. Has done so for centuries. There was little point in noting that despite being "handled," Klarissa still nearly succeeded in killing us. The mistake of magic that bonded me, a mortal female, to four immortal fae warriors still feels like a bard's tale to me —and even those don't always end well.

The mouthwatering smell of sizzling rabbit carries on the wind, guiding me to the morning meal. Our never-ending supply of game is a side benefit of traveling with four predators, one of whom prowls the night as a wolf. And not just the night.

I curse as I trip over a large, furry body lying across my path. "Is it really necessary to nap in the middle of a trail when there are acres of land around?" I ask Shade. If Coal won't tolerate touch outside training, threatens to crack my ribs, and generally makes himself scarce, Shade is his polar opposite: ever-present, cuddly, and as overprotective as a mother bear. Or mother wolf.

Shade yawns, opening his black muzzle wide to show an impressive set of teeth, and rises lazily to his feet. Pressing his front paws into the ground, he stretches his back. One way. Then the other way. Tail up, nose up. Then he shakes. With his sleek gray fur, powerful build, and sharp golden eyes, Shade's wolf is a sight to behold—and the furry bastard knows it.

"Oh, for stars' sake." I go to walk around the wolf, only to see a flash of light and find the male, now in fae form, silently falling in behind me.

"How was training?" Shade's arms capture my waist, forcing me to a halt against his smoothly muscled chest. His voice is a low caress across the top of my head that sends a delicious shiver through me, his body heat a blanket. "Are you hurt?"

"Only my pride."

"Mmm," Shade makes a noncommittal sound, his hands already moving over my skin, my arms, my shoulders, pressing gently against my ribs.

I twist around to face him. This version of Shade is even more distracting, with strong cheekbones and full lips, black hair swinging around his shoulders, and haunting eyes that seem to grow more intent on me with each passing day. "Nice as this is, you and I both know you are fussing. Blocking my path on happenstance is about as subtle as asking me questions to which you've no intention of believing the answers."

Shade blinks in offended innocence. "I'm not fussing. I'm simply aware of how rough Coal is with training."

I raise a brow, even as I savor the warmth spreading through me. No one has cared enough about me before to bother questioning my claims of wellbeing. After spending years as Zake's convenient mix of indentured servant and punching dummy, the quint's concern still sets me

7

ablaze. "So you do this with everyone after they train with Coal?"

Shade's innocence surrenders to a chuckle. "Only if I want my ass kicked. But I think you need a little more training before you pose a true danger to me, so I can indulge." Shade's hands slide to my face, the yellow eyes drinking in my gaze no longer a healer's, but a male's. He lets out a long, shuddering breath. "Does it bother you very much, cub?"

Leaning forward, I kiss Shade's cheek, his golden skin slightly prickly with stubble beneath my lips. "It's sweet. Just unnecessary."

Shade's jaw tightens, his throat bobbing as he swallows. "It is neither of those things," he says softly. "My wolf . . . My instinct to protect you grows by the day. It isn't easy to curb. Impossible altogether at times. I *am* sorry."

I bite my lip, my skin tingling as if a thousand little pricks of fire play along its surface. Despite the chill, Shade's cream shirt collar is open, revealing the hard swell of his pectoral muscles, the dip of his sternum. The leather laces whip like little flags in the wind. "I'm the only human in Lunos," I whisper. "A little protectiveness now and then is rather welcome."

"I'll remind you that you said that." Shade's calloused thumb traces my cheekbone. "You can still say no, cub," he whispers. "We are stepping into the Citadel today, but we aren't there yet. Now that you've had a chance to think . . . We'll understand if quint life isn't what you want. A mortal shouldn't be charged with defending Lunos and fae from Mors."

"I'm staying," I say firmly, my stomach clenching as Shade lets out a deep sigh of relief. "Of course I'm staying."

Shade's brow tightens. "There is a 'but' in there. I can smell it."

Damn fae and their bloody noses. Fine. "I don't want to be useless."

"You couldn't be useless if you tried, cub," Shade says with no trace of humor. "Your very presence gives us life. Stars. I wish I knew how to make you believe it."

I press my cheek into Shade's palm and he pulls me against him, his silky hair brushing his shoulder as he bows his head over mine. The smell of damp earth and rain fills my lungs, and my heart quickens in spite of itself, my hands rising to rest on Shade's taut hips. The yellow of his eyes shines in the sunlight, the bit of black in the center swallowing both the light and my thoughts. I wonder what those eyes see when they look at me from a wolf's body.

Shade's face dips down, his full lips parting in a way that turns the tingling along my skin into something feral. My body shivers, awakening with a steadily heating need that defies my command to stay put.

"Cub." Shade's voice rumbles from his chest, so soft that I feel rather than hear the sound.

My breath stills, my lungs no longer interested in air. Not when my mouth already tingles in anticipation—

"Breakfast?" Tye's voice wriggles between Shade and me.

We step apart, my face blazing. Shade gives the redheaded male a vulgar gesture.

Tye wraps his arm shamelessly around my shoulder and

looks down at me, his green eyes glinting in mischief, his sharp features spread into a grin. Up close, he's too handsome for his own good, and I scowl at him for it. "You must be starving, lass. Come eat while there is still meat left. We've Klarissa's mood to ruin today, and a millennium of Citadel tradition to turn upside down. Such endeavors are always better on a full stomach."

2

TYE

*T*ye smiled as he pulled Lera away from Shade, who was now staying back while he mastered himself. Had Tye's Lilac Girl found a way into River's or— by stars' own miracle—Coal's arms, he'd have given the pair their space. But Shade . . . Tye's grin deepened. It was simply too enjoyable to prod Shade now that the bastard was back in fae form and no stranger to the wonders of Lera's body.

Plus, Tye was doing Shade a service. Fae males were a protective and territorial lot to begin with, but Shade's wolf added a whole new level to the instinct. Shade was already laying claim to the girl, and Tye suspected that his wolf was trying to mate. If Tye's suspicion was correct, Shade would soon have a damn unpleasant battle on his hands in trying to maintain civility. Stars knew that Tye himself needed a dunk in cold water most mornings now to keep himself in check—and Shade would have it much worse.

Tye whistled a raunchy tune as he led Lera back to the breakfast campfire, pleasantly situated on the edge of a bluff overlooking the forested hills they'd trekked through. Far in the distance, a river glinted on the valley floor—the same river that ran all the way to Slait, emptying into the deep lake near the palace.

"Is there a reason you are so pleased with yourself, Tye?" River asked. The quint commander was checking the horses and gear, his dark eyes grave with planning their Citadel approach, his shoulders spread to carry the weight of responsibility—which he was more than welcome to, as far as Tye was concerned. Following orders was a great deal easier than giving them, and Tye was all about easy.

Like fine wine, life needed to be savored.

Lera wriggled away from Tye to wrap her hands around a mug of coffee sitting beside the flames, her curvy silhouette making Tye's heart beat just a little faster than normal. Tye was an expert in very few things . . . But when it came to females, his was a forte few others could match. Which qualified Tye to say, with authority, that Lera was like no one else in Lunos. Her sensuality went beyond that lush red-brown hair and creamy skin, those chocolate eyes that sent heat along Tye's veins. Even beyond her tight, gently swaying backside and breasts that peaked deliciously in the mountains' chill air. What made the lass unique lay somewhere in her soul and made her gaze at the world with eyes full of wonder and questions.

Maybe Lera's mortality had something to do with it, the

way she *lived* every moment and made those around her want to live it with her.

"Tye," River's low voice prompted.

Tye's eyes remained on Lera's backside as she straightened. "What's wrong with me being pleased with myself?"

"Because it is typically an indication that you've stolen something or are smuggling contraband," River said dryly.

Tye turned to his commander, who had paused in the middle of attaching a saddlebag to glare suspiciously at Tye. Yes, River oozed confidence and responsibility the way piranhas oozed slime. It was just an inseparable part of the prince of Slait Court that was always there, always awake, always braced to take on the weight of the world. Tye grinned, opening his arms to encompass the whole mountainside. "Where the bloody hell would I find something to steal around here?"

"That's what I want to know." River's eyes narrowed on a spot behind Tye, where Shade must have finally appeared. "Oh, for stars' sake, you two."

Blinking in innocence, Tye grabbed a skewer of rabbit meat from the flames.

The female blushed, ignoring them all and settling herself on a log. Her shyness. That was another one of Lera's delightful little sparks that Tye enjoyed stirring. Her body longed for touch, but often as not, her mind seemed to scold her for savoring the pleasure she deserved. Fortunately, between himself and Shade, Tye was certain they'd conquer that little barrier.

Tye's chest tightened. He'd had a chance to "conquer a

barrier" in a very literal sense a week ago. Finding herself alone with him for once, Lilac Girl had actually asked him to bed her. Being no stranger to the proposition—on either the asking or the receiving end—Tye still didn't fully understand why he'd said no, insisting on some nonsense about the whole quint being present. Lera didn't need the whole damn quint there for her first time.

Was it that he was afraid of hurting her—and quietly leaving that job to someone else? No. The first time could be rough on a female, but Tye knew he could make it worth her while. Prepare her until she was so wet and clenching with need that the pleasure of her release would swallow the sting. Make the hurt so good that it morphed into an ecstasy that had her screaming Tye's name.

Tye shifted his weight, the pressure in his cock growing from uncomfortable to downright painful with each colorful thought. Ripping his mind from Lera's phantom release— and his own matching pleasure—Tye forced himself to return to the question at hand.

Certainly, Tye wanted Lera. More than he'd ever wanted a female in his centuries of sampling them. He swallowed, his throat suddenly too narrow. Yes, that was it. His longing for Lera went beyond just bedding her. He wanted an exchange of intimacy that he'd not yet earned. Perhaps didn't deserve. Perhaps never would.

"So today is the day?" Lera said, handing her drained coffee mug to River for packing as Coal joined the group, his blond hair down for once and damp with lake water. "We go enter the Citadel and come out as the official, sanctioned quint that we already are? It seems like a lot of ceremony for little effect."

"As much could be said for wedding vows," Tye replied, though he sensed the ease of the lass's words was as much a lie as his own.

River shot him a glare then settled his gaze heavily on Lera. "This is a binding oath, not a formality. A pledge of obedience to the Citadel and a promise to protect Lunos."

Tye sighed. That was not the way to sell something—it was the way to chase a buyer off with a broom.

River's voice softened, making Tye dread the words he had no doubt his commander would say next. "Until the oath is spoken, you can still walk away, Leralynn. You *should* walk away. It would be the smart thing to do."

Lera crossed her slender arms over her chest, holding the commander's gaze in a way few immortals dared to. "And if I do, we would either need to sever the bond between us or all go live in the mortal lands?"

"Yes," River said.

"Then stop calling something a choice when it isn't, River," Lera said primly, snatching one of the meat skewers still remaining by the breakfast fire. Her teeth closed on a morsel of rabbit, pulling it delicately off the stick. "On a philosophical level, does it bother anyone that whoever the magic deigns to select for quint-ness must then bow to the Citadel? What if the chosen fae all want to be basket weavers, not warriors?"

Tye grabbed himself another meat skewer and dug out a wine cask from the saddlebags. Coffee was nice, but this conversation would go better with wine. Something dry and a bit tangy. "Mornings have become infinitely more entertaining since you joined our little gathering, Lilac Girl," he said around a mouthful of rabbit.

Shade gave Tye a warning look, a subtle show of rank from River's second-in-command.

River's jaw tightened, as it always did when he was forced to reconcile his personal dislike of the Elders Council with an equally potent loyalty to the Citadel's mission. "Flurry's, Slait's, and Blaze's court subjects must pledge an oath to their kings. This is little different. As for the magic selecting basket weavers, it's simply never happened. There is a warrior spark in every chosen being. The magic doesn't make mistakes."

"No?" Lera waved a hand over her very human self.

"You aren't a mistake," Tye said, getting to his feet and glaring at River. Heat pulsed through his veins as Autumn's words in the Slait palace library echoed in his memory. *Look at your quint now: a child of Slait, Blaze, Flurry, Mors, and now a child of the mortal lands. Doesn't that seem a bit too neat to be an accident?* But the female's research was only academic proof of what he'd already known in his gut.

"Tye." Shade's voice hardened. They were all falling into their hierarchical roles now, with the Citadel looming. Not that Tye much cared.

"Flurry," Tye said, pointing at the wolf shifter, before cycling through the other males. "Blaze. Slait. Mors. And now the mortal lands. Does that *seem* like a mistake to any of you?"

Silence settled over the quint, the others watching Tye warily as he panted, his hands opening and closing at his sides. Let them dare push him on this. Let them so much as try and Tye's tiger would feast on their flesh.

River cleared his throat, carefully taking a sip of wine before turning to address Lera. "We may not understand the magic's intentions, but you—"

"I connected with the four of you and survived," she said, smoothly taking River's sentence in her own direction. Her beautiful forehead tightened into a frown. "I think we should try it again before we enter the Citadel. Connect in a safe and controlled manner without anyone watching. See what we can do as a quint."

River choked on his drink. "Safe and controlled? That's akin to a safe and controlled fall off a bloody cliff."

Lera threw him a withering glance.

River studied her, his intelligent gaze incredulous. "Have you gone insane, Leralynn? Your surviving enough magic to kill most immortals was a bloody miracle—we are not going to tempt fate twice."

"Of course, River," Lera said in a too-sweet voice that woke every fiber in Tye's body to yet another realization. Last time the quint was at the Citadel, Tye and his elastic relationship with the law was River's greatest challenge to overcome. This time, that mantle would be going to someone else.

3

LERA

*W*e switchback up the steep road toward the Citadel, the hard-packed dirt granting good footing to the horses. My mare, Sprite, dances beneath me, sniffing the maples that are growing inexplicably greener the closer we get to the top. Magic. So much of it that even the trees and seasons bend to its will. A cacophony of birdsong rings from the branches around us, and flowering vines dangle from the branches arching over our heads. I wonder what the Gloom looks like here, whether I would still see the maples and large ash trees if we were to step into Lunos's dark undercurrent.

Not that I'm overly eager to find out.

My stomach tightens with each step, the Citadel rising above us like a white marble sentinel atop a forest-dressed mountain. I'd expected that the decision to remain a quint would bring a calm finality with it. The knot on a braid's end. It didn't. If anything, the knot is at the braid's beginning, with the weave still to come. With snags to be untangled along the way.

Focusing my mind on the current snag, I nudge Sprite to pull alongside River's dapple-gray stallion, who snorts excitedly.

"You'd be safer downwind." River pats his horse's neck. His spine is rod straight as always, the aura of unerring responsibility as much a part of his immortal princely self as his broad shoulders and gray eyes. The latter, all too used to making beings wither from a single glance. "Sprite is going into heat."

"All your centuries of training and you can't control your mount?" I say, maneuvering to the other side.

"I can control my mount just fine, Leralynn, but he is still a male and has instincts." He turns to me, those stormy eyes unnervingly intense. He frowns, his voice dropping to a murmur. "And he isn't the only one."

My skin heats. "Should I keep downwind of you as well?"

"No." River's eyes flick to the woods, where Shade trots along in his wolf form. The smooth planes of River's face tighten with worry. He pushes his horse in front of mine.

"What—"

A growl shatters the air before I can finish. With the next breath, Tye, River, and Coal surround me, their blades bared, muscles clenched in defense. My heart stutters at the sudden shift from casual conversation to deadly warriors, and I lick my lips to get moisture back into my mouth. Belatedly, I draw my own dagger, which Coal insisted on pinning to my waist. I feel just as ridiculous with the tiny weapon as I'm certain I look.

Shade's growl sounds again, and now I hear footsteps crashing through the forest. Whoever it is, they're no longer trying to shield their arrival from us. And then I see why, as one by one, five armed females emerge onto the trail, Shade snapping his teeth as he herds the procession. The front-most fae warrior, tall with cropped dark-brown hair and keen blue eyes, holds her head high as she approaches us. Like her four companions, she wears a fitted emerald-green tunic and black pants, with brown leather armor buckled over the cloth and vambraces of knives over her forearms. Now that I look closer, I see a single rune tattooed on her neck, just over her jugular. Hers and the other females' too.

A quint. Autumn told me that female groupings are rare, and I hadn't expected to run into one anytime soon. Though smaller than my males, the females' fierceness is so potent I can feel it crackling in the air. Tall, leanly muscled, and sun-kissed from long days in a training yard, they watch the forest, the road, and the five of us with unnerving intensity. Those who haven't cut their hair short like the leader's keep it in tight braids that twist and coil over their heads. Their eyes, to a one, are hard as flint.

"I presume that's your dog," the tall female says to River, who holds the point of the males' triangle. "Call him off, First Trial. Now. And sheathe your blades while you are at it." She surveys the four of us and Shade, who is sitting on his haunches now, his teeth still glistening in the sun. The female raises her chin. "I am Kora, a third-trial quint commander. We will take charge of you from here."

Tye snorts.

River shoots him a silencing look and sheathes his blade obediently before returning his attention to the females. "First Trial?"

Kora nods. "That is your rank," she says, her voice a mix of command and patience, like she's given this explanation countless times before. "As newly chosen initiates, you will be marked with three runes upon pledging your oath to the Elders Council. The runes symbolize the trials you must pass before you may leave Citadel grounds. As we," she gestures brusquely to the females flanking her, "have yet to complete our third trial, we are called 'third trials.' We are one trial away from being a recognized warrior quint, trusted to operate independently. Now, dismount."

"Who—" Tye starts to say, but River holds up a hand.

"Dismount," River says, his quiet voice more powerful than Kora's louder command. A flash of light has Shade shifting into his fae form, while I follow the others' example and slide to the ground. I can do it myself now, especially off Sprite, but it doesn't look nearly as smooth as the males' movements. River bows to Kora. "You were sent to meet us, I gather?"

Kora nods curtly. "We were told to expect a new quint— one with a female and four males." She frowns, her confident gaze growing wary as it brushes over us. River— tall, confident, hands clasped politely behind his back. Coal —arms crossed, glaring. Shade—stepping between me and the guards. Tye—silver earring glinting jauntily, green eyes moving from one female's chest to another. And me—human. In short, the males fit the description of wide-eyed initiates about as well as I fit one of an immortal warrior.

Kora clears her throat, her sword point dropping to the ground, coiled muscles relaxing slightly. "I apologize. I'd assumed you were the expected group before inquiring. If you might—"

"I imagine you have exactly the quint you were sent to meet," River says dryly. "And I look forward to meeting whoever sent you, just as soon as we enter the Citadel."

The points of Kora's ears turn a deep red as she sheathes her weapon. She opens her mouth then closes it again without speaking, as if none of the words that came to mind quite fit the situation. "You aren't first trials."

"No," River says gently. "Not for about three hundred years now. You were set up. I'm River."

Kora's eyes widen. "River, the prince of—"

"He has a large enough head without you reminding him of it, lass," Tye says, his hands in his pockets as he steps up casually beside me. "More importantly, I'm Tye, that is Coal, and you've already had the pleasure of meeting our puppy, Shade."

"Your quint is—"

"The second most powerful in Lunos, yes, we know," Tye says easily, shooting her a wink and wincing only slightly when Coal elbows him.

Kora bows, pulling her pride together with visible effort. Her eyes slide to mine. "And . . .?"

"And that is Leralynn, whom neither you nor anyone

else at the Citadel will go near." Shade's low voice is laced with venom, draining the blood from Kora's face and raising it in mine. Holding his ground between me and Kora, Shade is poised on the balls of his feet, his upper lip pulled back to show elongated canines. His shoulders, always wide, seem to have expanded further still to broaden his chest.

"Stand down, Shade," River orders softly, without so much as turning his head toward the male, before climbing back onto his stallion and bidding Kora to lead the way to the Citadel grounds.

I wait as Kora's quint falls in step beside River, and then I fall back to block Shade's path, my pulse pounding. "What the bloody hell was that?" I demand. *"That is Leralynn and you will not go near her?"*

Shade's jaw tightens. "That quint pointed weapons at you," he says finally, not meeting my eyes. "The fact that they walked away with their throats intact is a miracle in itself."

"One, that was rude." I poke my finger hard into Shade's chest, though my smaller frame dampens the effect. "And two, you don't have a say in who I choose to interact with."

Shade stands still, a thousand thoughts I can't read racing through his yellow eyes. No apology comes. No objection either. Just a flash of light before his wolf trots back into the forest.

4

COAL

*C*oal schooled his face to stone as they approached the mountaintop plateau, the dark clouds rushing overhead a mirror of his own thoughts. From here, all they could see was the immense marble wall encircling the Citadel, the pinnacle of the Elders Council's tower peeking out just above the white stone. Coal hated this place. The games and rules. The questions, most sent his way in silent, curious stares. *What was Mors like? Were you truly a slave? What did they make you do?* That last one, his own dreams answered for him too often. He didn't need to be reminded of it while awake as well.

A shiver rushed across Coal's skin, as it always did when walls and restraints loomed over him. An echo of another wall, cold and gray. Czar danced beneath him, the black stallion's ears lying flat as images raked through his rider's memories. *A jagged stone floor, sloped toward a drain in the corner.*

Tight manacles, rough with rust. Streaks of blood left behind by broken-off fingernails. The thick stench of pain.

Lera's gasp yanked him back so fiercely that the world swam for an instant. She was staring at him when it refocused, her chocolate eyes wide against her blanched skin, an acrid tang of fear washing off her.

As if she'd seen into his thoughts. His memories.

Coal's chest tightened, taking his breath. No, of course she hadn't. That was impossible.

Putting a hand on Czar's neck to quiet the stallion, Coal checked his voice before addressing the girl. Just being near her made him ache, and when she turned all her attention on him—like she was doing now—his heart had a habit of bolting like a high-strung colt. "Is something wrong, mortal?"

Lera blinked at him, the color slowly seeping back into her face, though her gaze remained too keen on his. "No." She shook herself. "No, it was . . . nothing."

"Good," Coal said tersely. Space. He needed space and fresh air that wasn't spiked with Lera's scent. "You should move downwind from Czar. Your mare—"

"Yes, River said as much." She put one hand on her hip. "Are you four going to go crazy when I bleed too?"

Coal's nostrils flared, smelling the female for hidden injury as his eyes surveyed her face, her body—her full chest and curves that the tight leather pants and belted tunic did nothing to hide. They all seemed all right. Lera certainly *had* been fully healthy when they trained this morning, her warm body pressing against every inch of Coal's until he was uncertain which of the two of them was in greater discomfort. If she was bleeding—

"Not now, you idiot." Lera rolled her eyes, her thick braid swinging against her back. "I mean, when I . . . go into heat."

Blood rushed to Coal's face. "I . . . I don't . . ." He had little notion of how often such things happened to humans. Glancing around for reinforcements, he found himself alone except for Tye, who'd plainly heard the question and was backing away before Coal could pull the bastard into the conversation.

"You are aware that such things happen, right?" Lera said.

"No. Yes." Czar danced beneath him again. Surrendering what little dignity he still had, Coal raised his face and bellowed for Kora, who had the decency to keep her face straight while listening to the problem. Once Coal was done speaking, however . . .

The laughter bubbling from Kora's chest started as a series of small, choked sounds, escalating to a full-chested howl before she could gather control over herself, her hands on her thighs. "Plainly"—she turned to Lera, whose own attempt at holding in her laughter was losing ground by the moment—"the answer is yes, they will go crazed whenever your cycle starts—seeing as how they can't even speak of it without turning red enough to signal their whereabouts to enemy troops."

Coal's jaw clenched. On top of everything, the mortal's form was starting to slip in the saddle, and Coal's hands strained with the desire to guide her shoulders and hips into alignment. "I'm glad you two find this so amusing."

"No," Lera tried and failed to master herself. "Not at all. It's just—"

"Stop," Coal said. "Just bloody stop. And get your heels down."

Swallowing a final laugh, Lera turned to Kora, now walking beside Sprite's shoulder. "Are you enjoying the Citadel?" she asked.

Kora gave Lera a sidelong glance, suspicion replacing amusement in her face.

Coal sighed. "No one *enjoys* the Citadel, mortal," he said, saving the trainee from having to choose between lying and speaking against her elders. "The trials and traditions are designed to be stressful and pit the quints against each other. With senior quints taking out the abuse they received at *their* elders' hands on the juniors, humiliation becomes a blood sport."

"Do many quints quit?" Lera asked. "I mean, after the trials? I know the runes stop anyone from leaving before then."

"Some," Coal said shortly. "No court will accept a rogue quint, so the defectors become a law unto themselves—or sell their services to the highest bidder."

"The Night Guard," Lera said slowly, her eyes squinting in memory.

"Yes." Coal straightened his back. They were almost at the Citadel gate now. "That is what those warriors siding with Mors's Emperor Jawrar and the qoru call themselves.

The council has dispatched us to put down several such units. Never a pleasant task."

"I imagine not," Kora said.

"Oh, come now," Tye cut in smoothly, blatantly nudging aside Coal's horse with his own.

Coal supposed it was a bloody miracle that the redheaded male had lasted this long before claiming the females' attention—though if Tye had eyes for Kora, he was likely barking up the wrong tree. Then again, since meeting Lera, Tye's appetites had turned very singular anyway.

"Bringing in rogues is better than disemboweling overgrown worms," Tye said. "River just happens to take it a wee bit too personally—being both the one exception to the 'no court will harbor a quint' rule *and* being rather high on the whole honor and duty thing."

"Could you translate what Tye just said, please?" Lera asked, her eyes sending lightning down Coal's spine.

"River is the prince of Slait," Coal said, pointedly not looking at the commander. "If his father dies, River will ascend the throne and Slait will thus absorb our quint."

Tye grinned. "Understandably, the Elders Council wants River on Slait's throne—and free of their control—about as much as River's father wishes to die off."

"*Enough,*" River ordered sharply, pointing ahead. They'd rounded the final switchback, and now the wall rose above them, blindingly white in the sun. The wide road led through an intricate metal archway that stood taller than two fae males and now opened on silent hinges before them.

Coal knew that it would shut just as silently and implacably behind them when they went through it.

5

LERA

I dismount before going through the gate. Not because Sprite would have any trouble navigating the entrance, but to buy myself a few extra moments. Despite the laughter and conversation, echoes of the haunting images that flooded my mind at the first sight of this wall still thud through me. *Gray, cold, streaked with blood left by broken fingernails. Manacles cut into my skin, the sound of them closing around my wrists turning my bowels. The stench of pain to come*—I blink to disperse the vision.

Shade's wolf hangs back to wait for me. Then, catching my eye, he seems to think better of it and lopes on after the others, letting me find my own footing through the gate.

Whatever dungeon I thought I saw in my mind, I discover a moment later, was most certainly *not* the Citadel. Grand buildings of shining white marble rise in every direction, connected by a vast square of geometric pathways and manicured, bright green grass. Flowing grapevines wrap around thick columns. The air smells like fruit blossoms and freshly cut lawn. Fae stride along with purpose, some—armed and uniformed in a manner similar to Kora and her warriors—moving together in groups of five. Others, dressed in whatever struck their fancy that morning, stride alone or in pairs, their arms laden with books and scrolls. I'd imagined the Citadel as a military barracks of sorts, but it appears to be a place of study and learning as much as a warrior training ground. How I imagine a university would look back in the mortal lands, not that I've ever stepped close to one.

"Stars," I breathe, surrendering Sprite into the care of a hostler who has appeared silently to tend to the horses. "This place is gorgeous."

River and Coal exchange a glance that I can't read, Tye suddenly finding the cuffs of his jacket incredibly interesting.

Discomfort slithers through me, but before I can question the males, River steps in front of Kora. "I wish to meet whoever told you that first trials were coming and sent you to intercept us."

Kora's face colors. "It was a misunderstanding, sir."

"It was a calculation meant to humiliate you," River says flatly. "I am quite familiar with the quint-trainee hierarchy, Kora. Including the power that senior trainees have to issue orders to their juniors. I presume this specific instruction came from a third trial who's senior to you?"

The female lifts her chin. "A misunderstanding."

"I wasn't making a request," River says, with enough quiet force to make Kora's skin blanche.

"Yes, sir." Kora bows, drawing herself up again. "Malikai and his quint will most likely be in the practice arena at this time of day. It's this way."

The female quint starts walking and I go to follow, only to realize that my body is little eager to obey. Filled with fae warriors and grand structures and magic, the breathtakingly beautiful Citadel suddenly seems like a poisonous flower. A spark of envy tugs at my chest as I watch Kora's confident steps. A warrior in body, heart, and soul. And me . . . I try to swallow, finding my mouth so dry that I fail even at that.

When the Elders Council sees me, they are going to roll on the floor in laughter.

A small nip of pain pulls my attention to my hand, currently in the mouth of a large wolf, his tail swaying slowly beside my left thigh. River, Coal, and Tye, I realize a moment later, have closed ranks around me as well. All trying to look like they wandered into the formation by sheer accident. I take a deep breath, inhaling River's clean, woodsy scent, spiced with the pine, earth, and metallic musk of the others, a blend that's as familiar now as it is comforting.

"Thank you," I whisper, feeling even more grateful when not a single one acknowledges having heard me. We move out to follow Kora across the broad central square, toward a building shaped like a cistern, a wide, circular structure with a flat top.

"You realize that this Malikai bloke could only have

31

POWER OF FIVE BOOK 2 & BY ALEX LIDELL

known we were coming if he's licking the council's boots," Tye says softly.

"The council's favorite trainees have always been the worst," River says, his hands clasped behind his back. Stars know how he managed it, but the blue jacket and black pants he donned this morning still look as crisp as new. "I can't imagine that's changed."

I try to mimic the male, straightening my back and lowering my tensed shoulders in what I'm certain are subtle movements—until Tye groans on my right.

"Him? Of all of us to take after, you chose that ugly bastard?" he demands.

The bastard in question turns to flash his glistening canines at Tye. "What did you expect? Leralynn is much too bright to take after you."

"Tell me what all these buildings are," I say quickly, halting the retort I can see forming on Tye's tongue. "I assume the tall tower is for the council, but what is that huge bowl beneath, with the paddock beside it?"

"That's the trial arena," River says, smoothly accepting the change of subject. "It is heavily warded and only accessible during trials. A smaller practice arena, where we're headed now, and other training structures line the north side of the Citadel. The dormitories for quints, visiting scholars, and staff are on the south end. The large building on the east corner is the library, with the dining hall beside it."

"What about that sea of huts?" I say, squinting against the high sun as I point south toward a distant cluster of wooden buildings that seem to belong to this sacred place as little as I do.

"Guard country," River replies, his voice tight. "That's where non-bonded warriors like Pyker dwell. They keep to themselves there, unless on duty."

Pyker. Klarissa's pet, who tried to stage my death and come out the hero. I want to ask where he might be now, having been handed back into Klarissa's hands a week ago, but we are already walking up to the smaller cistern-shaped building. Up close, I can see that it's a broad, windowless stone tower with a set of steps winding around the outside wall from ground to roof.

Except there is no roof, I realize as the ten of us get to the top—just the flat edge of a thick wall encircling a sand floor two stories below. Two groups of five fae males are there now, both sets dressed similarly to Kora's quint except for their underlying colors—a fiery orange and a mute purple instead of the females' emerald green.

The orange quint stands with their hands connected, a glow like a miniature sun surrounding the five of them. And the purples . . . I wince as an invisible force lifts two of the males into the air and slams them into the wall. The orange leader, a tan-skinned male with long black hair tied back at the nape of his neck and a sharp widow's peak, laughs. Even at this distance, his pale eyes glow cruelly from his handsome face. "Get up and do it again," he calls as his victims gather themselves, blood covering their skin, hair, and clothes.

Bile rises in my throat. I've seen this scene before. Lived it. Not the magic and uniforms and training arena, but the sheer helplessness of a larger master doling out punishing blows that, no matter what he or anyone says, nothing will prevent.

A hand spreads on my back. Not along one of the spots that the males' palms often brush—my shoulders or lower waist—but right under a shoulder blade. Where Zake's belt left its final marks before the males pulled me from that stable.

I turn my head to find Coal there. Not looking at me at all, even as his touch says everything.

"That is Malikai?" River asks Kora. "The senior of the third trials?"

"Yes, sir," the female says grimly. Her body is tense, uncomfortable with being here. "But those are first-trial trainees. The newest."

I swallow, my voice low enough for only Coal to hear. "If River calls out Malikai now, the bastard will make Kora pay for it later."

Coal says nothing.

Before I can say more, one of the purples holds out his hands, a fireball launching from his palms. I gasp, jerking away from the edge and into another male body.

Tye puts an arm around my shoulder, his pine-and-citrus scent soothing my nerves. "The practice arena is warded," he says into my ear. "The magic will not escape these walls."

The fireball slams into the orange quint's shimmering shield, the flame dissolving into harmless hissing smoke. In retaliation for the assault, rocks the size of small apples rise from beneath the sand, pelting the purple fire-thrower until he cries out, collapsing to his knees.

"Again," Malikai calls to the fire-thrower, who is still down on all fours. "Do you imagine your first arena trial will be gentler? Maybe you should beg the council to cleave you idiots apart now. Save us all the trouble."

I don't see Coal move until he is flying through the air to land softly in the middle of the sparring ring. With his tight black leathers, fierce blue gaze, and long sword strapped down the groove of his back, he is the consummate warrior. Beside him, the other fae seem little more than colorful toys.

"Who the bloody—" Malikai's words die in midair as he finds himself looking first at Coal and then at the rest of us, lining the top of the stone wall. When Malikai's gaze touches mine, his eyes flash with distaste. Turning back to Coal, however, the male pulls himself up straight and bows, the rest of the males on the sand following his example. "Sir," he says, his tone full of grudging subservience, "how might we be of assistance?"

"I want this space," Coal says calmly.

"Of course." Malikai bows again, his face tight. "We will clear out at once. My apologies for not anticipating your needs."

I raise a questioning brow at River. "Seriously? Did that bastard just go from thinking himself a god to pretending to be a footman in a heartbeat's time?"

River nods without humor. "Coal is a full quint warrior and Malikai only a third trial. He has no choice, not unless he wishes to find himself at the flogging post."

Of course the Citadel would have such a thing. A poisonous flower indeed.

Coal's hand shoots out, grabbing Malikai's wrist. "Keep your quint here, Third Trial," he says in that velvet-soft voice that promises painful things to come. "I wish to train."

A corner of River's mouth twitches, the only sign he gives of having an opinion on Coal's actions.

Malikai swallows. "Of course. It will be our pleasure to provide whatever your quint—"

"Not my quint." Coal's smile is feral as he pulls his sword from the scabbard down his spine. The razor-sharp steel winks in the sun. "Just me."

My heart stutters. Five. Coal wants to go up against five.

The purple quint is out of the arena in the blink of an eye, climbing up a ladder I didn't notice before and bowing to us as they slide by toward the outside steps.

"All of us," Malikai clarifies with Coal down below, his voice growing cockier. "Again, just—"

That's as far as he gets before Coal's heel sweeps the back of Malikai's ankle and the male lands hard on the sand.

Behind Coal, Malikai's quint brother gathers a ball of orange flames around his hand. I open my mouth to shout a warning, but River touches my arm and motions for silence. My heart pounds as the flaming sphere grows to the size of a grapefruit and the male holding it cocks his arm to throw the mass at Coal's unprotected back.

At the last moment, Coal moves, his muscles flexing like a dancer's as his body slides off the center of the attack.

The fireball, deprived of its intended target, continues on, now rushing toward the half-risen Malikai.

The orange-clad male drops gracelessly back to the sand, narrowly avoiding the blazing magic, which fizzles harmlessly against the far wall.

Coal is already rolling again, avoiding a second blazing sphere, this one lobbed against the hissed advice of the other warriors. Coal's steel glistens in the sun as he comes to his feet, a stone gripped comfortably in his free hand. One of the damn rocks that Malikai's quint pelted the first trials with. My breath halts as Coal's arm snaps like a whip, each muscle so perfectly controlled as to make the movement seem slow motion. The stone flies from his palm, cracking into the fire-thrower's hand.

The male screams and bends over his bloodied limb, his pain and fury echoing off the arena's stone walls while the third fireball he'd been building fizzles into smoke.

"Connect!" Malikai orders, his quint brothers already rushing to the downed fire-thrower, their hands outstretched.

My stomach clenches. A connection. The moment those five link together—

Coal flows. A blur of leather and steel as he rises suddenly at the head of the column that Malikai's quint scampers to form. Forcing the quint's males to be in each other's way.

Malikai, who was the farthest from the column, rushes forward with his arm outstretched—only to yank it back as Coal's sword slices the air that Malikai's hand was about to travel through.

Grabbing that arm, Coal twists it behind Malikai's back hard enough to drive the male to his knees. With the next heartbeat, Coal's sword rests against Malikai's exposed windpipe, the defeated male's chest heaving with deep, ragged breaths.

"Anyone make a move and I will slit your commander's throat," Coal informs the quint calmly.

They freeze, looking to their kneeling leader for instruction until Malikai manages to rasp, "Yield," nicking his own throat on Coal's blade in the process.

Withdrawing the sword, Coal shoves Malikai between the shoulder blades, sending the male's face into the sand. "Get up and let's do this again," Coal says, now swinging his weapon in a lazy arc. "I've all the time in the world."

6

RIVER

*R*iver gave Coal an hour to work off his aggression before reining in the male. In truth, River would have gladly let Coal wipe the sand with Malikai all bloody day, but they could keep the Elders Council waiting for only so long.

As it was, by the time the five of them descended from the practice arena, a footman was already waiting impatiently to show them to a chamber where they could change and freshen up before attending the waiting council.

"You absolutely cannot go in your fighting leathers," River growled at Coal, who'd been leaning against the wall as if the process in no way involved him.

"At least I have pants on," Coal jerked his chin at Tye, who appeared to have forgotten about his own clothing as he watched Leralynn negotiate the formal dress Autumn had packed for her.

The luscious blue satin fit the girl's curves with sinful perfection, its skirts full and shifting like water in the light slanting through the windows. Rows of tiny diamonds accented the tight bodice and flowered down the back, where the material narrowed to a sparkling column along Leralynn's spine. The delicate cut of her shoulder blades peaked like wings beneath her smooth skin.

River swallowed, throwing cold water over his face in an effort to release the sudden tightness in his breeches. Shade's low chuckle dispelled River's hopes that the moment had gone unnoticed.

By the time the five approached the tower, the council's patience had grown so thin that one of them was waiting outside. And not just anyone.

River stepped in front of Leralynn as the five approached Klarissa, who stood elegantly on the steps of the marble tower, her painted lips as bright as glowing embers. Despite being dressed in an elder's formal robes, Klarissa was as feminine as always, the champagne diamond on her finger—the same color as her flowing silk robe—failing to melt her icy gaze. The sun, bouncing off the white stone at her back, created an aura of light around the female and played off the golden thread woven into her dark chignon.

And yet . . . Leralynn's untamable waves of fiery hair somehow gave her a deliciously raw quality, a rugged sensuality that made Klarissa's cold perfection feel stale in comparison.

"You do us too great an honor, meeting us outside the tower, Elder," River said with a bow.

"I feared you might have forgotten the way," Klarissa replied, her alto voice as musical as it was callous.

"How is wee Pyker?" Tye drawled casually, swaggering up on Klarissa's other side. "Has the council tried him yet for treason?"

River swallowed a groan. Needling Klarissa, as damn good as it felt, was squarely outside the realm of "smart things to do" when going before the council. Not that prudency had ever stopped Tye from doing something before.

Klarissa's hard eyes cut to the redhead, who blinked innocently. "Unfortunately, the rogue took his own life before justice could be served."

"Indeed," River said dryly. Now that Tye had started this conversation, there was little use in pretending they'd expected anything different. A death or two had never presented an obstacle to Klarissa's agenda before, and there was no reason to expect it would now. River's heart thumped a hard, even beat. The sooner they could get Leralynn away from the Citadel, the better he'd feel.

Draping his arms loosely behind his back, River followed Klarissa's swaying hips up the four hundred seventy-seven steps lining the inside of the tower's walls. The rhythmic click of the female's heels against stone beat a contrast to Leralynn's increasingly labored breathing behind him. River looked back. *Stars.* He forced his eyes away from the girl before all the blood in his body left his mind to visit more primal regions. Still, if he could just lift her into his arms and carry her up the steps . . .

"She wouldn't like it," Coal murmured at his back, too keenly for River's comfort.

River grunted noncommittally. Why under all the stars the mortal female measured her physical prowess against theirs, he couldn't fathom. Leralynn brought life to the quint —no one needed her to bring muscle to it too. They had more than enough brawn to go around.

Reaching the landing outside the council's chamber, River let Klarissa go ahead while he and the others waited for Shade and Leralynn to catch up. The males had slowed in deference to Leralynn's pace, but River could still smell the blood rushing too quickly beneath her blushing skin, her breathing harsh in her chest, her light dusting of freckles more pronounced than usual.

Stopping on the landing beside River, Leralynn braced her hand on the wall and smiled at him bravely, her dimples making his heart clench.

Shouldering Coal out of the way, Shade put the flat of his palm against the small of Leralynn's back in a too-casual gesture that neither River nor any of his quint brothers missed. Leralynn stiffened, her eyes widening as her panting eased, her skin returning to its natural color.

"A useful trick," she murmured to Shade, who raised his brows in a plea of innocence.

River longed to touch the girl as well, just to reassure himself that Leralynn was in fact real and there and all right. His heart quickened as he took a step toward her. Stars. River was over five hundred years old, and somehow, closing the three-pace distance to Leralynn frightened him more than any battle. It was absurd. It was stupid. It was—

It was too late. River stepped aside as Tye beat him to it, putting his hands on Leralynn's face and brushing a soft kiss right over those luscious lips.

"Just in case you'd forgotten about me, lass," Tye said, his cocky voice filling the landing. "Not that it's likely."

"It's time to go," River said, more roughly than he'd intended. He turned and reached for the chamber's large door. The sooner they walked in there, the sooner they could leave.

The Elders Council chamber was undeniably grand, a circular room lined with tall, arched windows and covered in a series of vibrant murals depicting the fae leaving Mors and creating Lunos. Golden trim lined each window and the edge of the domed ceiling, which rose to a small circular skylight two stories above. A single table on a raised dais in the center was carefully positioned to bathe the elders in the rays of sunlight flowing through the windows. It was an impressive set-up designed to project an image of divine power, but River had been here often enough to know that the elders rotated the table as the sun traveled across the sky, the radiant light little more than a well-made calculation.

Like Klarissa, the others wore voluminous silk robes, each in his own color. Blood red, deep green, sapphire blue, and—for the head elder and quint commander, sitting in the center chair—midnight black. The elders' silhouettes cast long shadows along the floor, stretching over the marked line where solicitors were to stand. The most powerful quint in Lunos. And, until now, the only mixed-gender one.

Stepping up to the well-worn line, River spread his feet shoulder-width apart, bowing his head respectfully while the others fell into line beside him, Shade and Tye flanking Leralynn. The girl was most comfortable with the shifters, who were healthier for her than River could ever be. As he watched, Leralynn's eyes narrowed on the elders' shadows, then slipped along the floor in search of something—marks of wear, most likely. So she'd figured out the light trick already. Smart girl.

"The meeting of the Elders Council of the Citadel will come to order," said the tall black-robed male in the raised middle seat, his voice booming off the domed ceiling. The silver hair hanging loose to the male's shoulders concealed part of a jagged scar that narrowly missed his right eye. He gripped a palm-sized stone sphere and struck it against a carved wooden cradle on the table before him. That thud, too, echoed. "I am Elder Beynoir, the head of the council. With me are Elders Vallyann, Klarissa, Hairan, and Elidyr. Standing before the dais are River of Slait, Shade of Flurry, Tye of Blaze, Coal, and a mortal female."

"Leralynn," the girl said suddenly, flinching as the marble dome amplified her voice.

Tye—who bloody well should have known to keep his mouth shut—snorted softly.

"Your pardon?" Beynoir frowned down at her, as if surprised to discover that the mortal had the power of speech. In his defense, most immortals tended to lose said power upon walking into this chamber and grasping the council's power over them.

"My name, sir." This time, at least, Leralynn bowed. "It seems more efficient to call me Leralynn, rather than 'that mortal female' over and over again."

Elder Elidyr, sitting in his green robe at the opposite end of the table from Klarissa, suppressed a smile. With a lively oval face and thick brown hair plaited down the back of his neck, Elidyr had always been more comfortable sitting in a saddle than a chair, and he was the one council elder whose support and fairness River could count on absolutely. But Elidyr was only one of five.

Beynoir shifted in his seat, his black robes rippling in stark contrast to his light hair. "Yes, thank you." His voice rose. "I understand that you five have come to request assistance in severing the tether between the fae and the mortal—Leralynn." Beynoir paused to incline his head at her. "Such that Leralynn might return to the safety of the mortal lands while the fae remain able to reclaim the full power of their quint."

In the corner of his eye, River saw Leralynn's mouth open and shot her a warning glance that she, by some miracle of the stars, obeyed. "I fear you've been misinformed, Elder Beynoir," River said crisply into the silence. "The magic has chosen a fifth warrior to complete my quint. We come before the council not to shatter the bond, but to renew our oath." He paused, carefully keeping his gaze on Beynoir alone. "We informed Elder Klarissa of this a week ago."

Beynoir frowned. "Klarissa?"

The female waved a slender hand, her champagne diamond flashing on her finger. "I little wished to prejudice you against them in hopes that common sense, duty, and safety would have prevailed before they arrived here. It appears, however, that I've given these five more credit than they are due."

Beynoir's brows narrowed at River, his hooked nose dominating his scarred face. "A mistake of magic has been made. Am I to understand that instead of correcting it, you wish to follow this error to its inevitable chaotic end and pledge a quint's oath with the bonded human?"

"Yes, sir," River said.

"Ridiculous." Klarissa's gaze focused on her nails. "A mortal cannot complete a quint. It is fortunate the council is here to intervene when young males think with organs other than their brains, Elder Beynoir."

"If the council intervened every time a male's cock got in the way of common sense, we'd have no time for anything else, Klarissa," Elidyr said from the opposite side of the table, thoughts already racing in his intelligent eyes. "And I recall much the same once being said of us, for our mixed-gender bond. I'll say now what I said then—the *magic* chooses the quints, not the council."

"We are all fae, Elidyr," Klarissa said. "This girl is human. It is absurd to pit her against Mors, and I submit that the council cannot set a precedent for absurdity."

Elidyr opened his wide palms, his thick braid swaying as he turned to address the head elder directly. "The wisdom of the quint's request is immaterial. The bond cannot be severed without the consent of all five quint members, unless one of them faces imminent death. I thus see little point in this discussion."

"On the contrary"—Klarissa raised her chin, flashing a triumphant glance at River—"if these beings insist on tying themselves to a mortal, they can go to the mortal lands with her."

"Enough." Beynoir knocked the stone sphere against its wooden cradle, quieting the room. Seconds passed as the elder gazed down at the quint, tracing his scar with one long finger, each heartbeat tightening his jaw further. "I agree with Klarissa," he said finally, the words echoing in the silence. "Pitting a mortal against the qoru will unduly endanger her and Lunos both. You five are playing into an accident, and that is not something I will condone."

Ice rushed down River's spine. "Sir—"

Beynoir raised a hand. "I may be unable to force you to sever the bond, but I need not make accommodations for you, either. You may, as Klarissa suggested, leave the Citadel's neutral lands. Otherwise, you will be required to enter the Citadel as a new quint, and shall be treated as such."

For the first time since walking into the chamber, River's voice faltered. "You would have us start over as a new quint, sir?" he asked. "As first-trial initiates? After three hundred years of experience?"

"You have no years of experience being bonded to a mortal, River," Beynoir snapped. "Other re-bonded quints are granted their former status as a matter of courtesy, not law. If you would like to remain in Lunos, you will *all* submit to the Citadel's rules. Bare your skin to receive the trial runes, or leave Lunos. Those are your choices."

Behind River's back, his grip on his own wrist tightened so hard, his hand fell asleep. He and the other fae could face the trials again, weather the humiliations poured onto initiates, fight their way out before Klarissa's training succeeded in ending one of their lives. But Leralynn. *Stars.* It wasn't worth it. Nothing was worth putting her through that. Turning to the girl, River shook his head.

Leralynn watched him for a moment, her beautiful brown eyes filled with warmth—and apology. Before River could move to stop her, she raised her face, turning directly to Beynoir. "Where do the runes go, sir? I'm ready to receive them, but I could use some instruction."

7

LERA

he weight of all eyes turned on me is as heavy as the council chamber's echo, but it is only River's gaze that I return. His square jaw is clenched, his gray eyes tight, his broad shoulders braced to bear the weight of all the stars—or rally a force against them. River's stance alone marks him a prince, as if he has shed some cloak he wore on his power and now lets it flame brightly.

No wonder Klarissa cannot let him be.

"Might we have a moment, Elders?" River says, turning his attention back to the dais.

A small smile touches the corners of Klarissa's lips, while Elder Beynoir nods toward the door.

Except I don't need River's moment, don't want him doubting my choice. I raise my chin, hoping my silence is message enough.

"Leralynn." A command from River, who either didn't

see or little cared for my resolve. When I fail to move again, the male grasps the top of my arm, leaving me with the choice of walking out on my own two feet or being dragged.

I opt for the former, though my heart pounds so hard, it's all I can do to keep from growling at River, at least until we step out onto the landing. "What the bloody stars was that?" I demand, wheeling on him the moment the door shuts. "You think I'm some sort of child to be marched out of a room?"

"I think you've no notion of what you are agreeing to." River's cold calm sends a fresh wave of fury through me. "Once those runes sear into your skin, they stay there until all three trials are completed. There is no second guessing."

I rock forward on my toes, tipping my head back to stare into River's storm-filled eyes. The air between us thickens, as if readying itself for lightning. "Then stop second guessing me," I tell him, the words escaping clenched teeth. I raise my hand, my index finger striking the middle of his hard chest. "I choose the quint, River. And if this is the price, then I *want* to pay it."

River grabs hold of my wrist, small as a sprite's in his large, calloused hand. His shoulders spread like wings, claiming all the space around us. "Stop being bloody brave, Leralynn. The trials have killed greater fae than—"

"I don't care." My voice finally cracks. I turn my wrist in his grip and cup his cheek, warm skin rough with new stubble. River's eyes flare. "I don't care what they are, or how we get through them. We fight for each other, all right?"

The tension slowly leaves River's shoulders but his eyes remain worried.

I take his arms, give him one soft shake, though it's like trying to shake a boulder. "All right?" I say again, softer now. A caress of words along his ragged gaze.

Closing his eyes, River leans down, touching his velvet lips to my forehead and sending a web of warmth tingling along my skin and soul.

We walk back into the chamber together, River holding the door open for me before following my steps toward the line of others.

Klarissa smiles.

River's gaze cuts to Shade, Coal, and Tye in turn, the males exchanging subtle but certain nods, before River finally faces the council. "We agree to your terms, Elders," he announces clearly. "We stand before you as a new quint, requesting initiation into the Citadel."

The smile dies, Klarissa's olive skin flushing a deeper hue that plays off her brown eyes. "Then kneel, initiates. You do not stand in the presence of council elders."

River sinks obediently to his knees, his back and face remaining tall. The others and I follow River's example, though it looks less than graceful on my part—and positively edged with murderous violence on Coal's.

The rough stone shreds my knees, the impact of the fall vibrating through my bones. My shackled arms are pinned behind my back, the manacles—there are no manacles. No rough stone. No pain. I'm in a marble council chamber, and one of the elders is speaking again, his voice penetrating the momentary haze even as I stare at my males, my heart breaking. I've made them drop to their knees, these proud warriors who've fought for three hundred years.

"Is this truly necessary?" Elidyr says. "I understand the desire to test this quint before sending it out into the field, but do we need to insist on formalities designed to discipline new warriors? The males standing—kneeling—before us would make better instructors than students."

"We must insist on formalities now more than ever," Beynoir counters. "These five have already proven themselves ready to make a mockery of our ways. They shall be treated as all other trainees are." Beynoir raises his hand, now glowing bright as a hot iron. "The initiates may come up to receive their marks."

Stars.

"Come here, River," Klarissa's silky voice orders.

I watch, my breath catching in my throat, as the prince rises to his feet and strides to the female, baring his neck to her flaming touch. Fear cold enough to seize my spine holds me in place, my heart leaping into a racing, tripping gallop.

"Come here, Leralynn." Beynoir's voice pierces my chest, even as I hear the others summon their respective victims. "Leralynn?"

I rise, my beautiful blue dress giving me no more courage than rags would have. My hands tremble and I nearly trip over my own feet while taking the five steps to the dais. But I do take them, and I present myself before the elder, my chin held high despite my pounding pulse.

Beynoir's hand is gentler than I expected as he tilts my head and moves my thick hair off the side of my neck. His finger brushes my skin, and for a second I think that the flame I saw was little but an illusion. Perhaps whatever is about to happen—

My thoughts scatter as a hot brand presses against my neck, the stench of burning flesh making bile mix with my echoing screams.

Beynoir's free hand rushes forward, grabbing my shoulder before I can fall. The brand still presses into me, a white-hot agony. The runes don't just burn my skin—they scourge everything inside me as if forging a chain of flaming iron that runs all the way into my heart. Even with the support of the elder's arm, my knees buckle, the world fading in and out of focus in bursts of pain.

"This is off to a grand start," Klarissa says, though it's a miracle anyone can hear the female's words over my howl.

A snarl echoes through the domed chamber, the smell of fur filling my lungs right before powerful arms pull me against a familiar, taut body. "I have you," Shade says, his voice tight. "I have you." The male's cool palm rests between my shoulder blades, a thin thread of magic rippling through me, coaxing my lungs to fill with air.

I try to smile at the image, but it comes as a wince.

Shade tips my head slightly, his touch featherlight along the still-throbbing marks. "A knot woven of four cords. Interesting. The first time around, we had a jackrabbit."

"Initiates of the Citadel"—Beynoir's voice is a bare rumble over Shade's scent—"welcome to the start of your training. I will assign a senior quint to assist you in getting settled and learning—or ignoring—the rules. I would ask for questions at this point, but I imagine that at least three of you are familiar enough with the Citadel and its rules to be able to lead the lecture yourself."

"Three?" The word is out of my mouth before I can catch it.

"There is some debate as to whether Tye is incapable of understanding rules or simply cannot fathom a reason to follow them," Beynoir says dryly. "But do not worry, young Leralynn. What that male lacks in comprehension of rules, he makes up for in comprehension of penalties. In short, it is fortunate that one of your quint mates has a healing gift." The elder raises his face to survey our group. "Now, if there are no additional matters to address—"

River takes a step forward and bows. "There is one matter, sir. If the council will indulge me."

The sphere in Beynoir's hand lowers back without making a sound, and the elder sighs. "Yes?"

"My quint requests to face its first trial immediately."

8

LERA

*I*mmediately turns out to be tomorrow morning, with Klarissa, of all beings, insisting that the five of us at least get a full night's sleep before stepping into the arena.

Putting on a brave front, I follow River and the others out the door to the never-ending spiral staircase, making it all of three steps before a pair of strong arms lifts me into the air. Shade's earthy scent fills my nose as he cradles me against his hard chest, his cheek resting on the crown of my head.

I wriggle. "I can walk."

"I can't," Shade says, pulling me closer to his chest, which feels like steel wrapped in velvet under my cheek. His heart is beating hard enough that I feel its vibrations. Shade takes a deep whiff of my scent. "I need you here just now, cub. Please."

My protests die away, my fingers tracing the three runes on his neck, the marks that have just burned our commitment into the fabric of the world. The bard's tale made real. Around us, Tye, Coal, and River keep a tighter pattern than usual. The latter doing such a good job not looking at me that he might as well be staring.

Reaching the bottom landing, River opens the door, propelling the five of us into the bright sun. My head spins as Shade reluctantly sets me on my feet, the enormity of the past quarter hour hitting me as brightly as the light. What in the bloody stars have I done, swearing to be a warrior that I can never become? A shiver runs down my spine. What if we never leave the Citadel, the males trapped here like caged animals because of me?

"I can live with a few weeks here," Tye says, sticking his hands in his pockets. Shaking his red hair to try—and fail—to clear it from his eyes, he gives me an encouraging grin, his voice forcibly light. "Citadel grapes make some of the best wine in Lunos. A few words in the right—"

"Stop talking." Coal glowers at Tye before twisting to face me, his clear blue eyes seeming to penetrate my thoughts. "We will train, mortal. And we *will* walk out of here. All of us."

"We'll train between now and tomorrow morning?" My voice rises in spite of itself and I must stop to force air into my lungs. I wrap my arms tightly around myself.

River turns, his voice too damn matter-of-fact. "The first trial is a quint-versus-quint challenge that tests a new group's ability to work together. With three centuries of experience, I don't imagine a few more weeks would make a notable difference."

"*You* have three centuries of experience," I say. "I have two weeks. Flattered as I am that you imagine I can battle five immortals, I'm not sure Coal would agree."

"I don't," Coal confirms. "Which is why you won't be doing any of the fighting."

"Coal is right, cub," Shade says, rubbing his warm hands down my bare shoulders. "You've been brave enough. Let us take care of tomorrow."

"Is there someone else coming out that door after you?" The familiar female voice makes me jump as Kora steps up to the group. Her short dark-brown hair is tucked behind one pointed ear, which, I notice for the first time, bears a tiny emerald stud. "Or am I finding myself at the ass end of a second jest today?"

"I see Klarissa is as efficient as ever," River murmurs, tilting his head to show Kora the runes. "If you are looking for the first trials you've been assigned to herd, then you've found them."

Kora stares at River's neck, then his face. "That is asinine, sir," she says finally. "If you'll forgive my language."

"I've heard worse," River says. "You should also get out of the habit of using that title, Kora, given that you are our superior now—we all have enough of a mess on our hands without violating the Citadel's proprieties."

Kora sighs, shaking her head. "Well, let's take you on the introductory tour."

⌇

"I EXPECTED a barren room with stacked wooden cots," I say, running my hand over upholstered walls rich enough to give the Slait Palace competition. The suite our quint has been assigned has its own entrance on the bottom floor of a long two-story building, complete with a thick, ornately carved wooden door and a small, rose-bush-lined walkway. The suite itself has five sleeping chambers, four on one side of a common room and one—which Coal immediately claimed for himself—on the other. The armchair I sink into is soft and finely made, and someone has built a cheery fire in the hearth. "Is this not a bit . . . excessive?"

"It's a message, like everything else," River says, settling on the wide leather couch, the low mahogany table before it laden with fruit, cheese, and delicate finger sandwiches. "Power of opposites. Show the quints they are elite, but must bow completely to the Citadel's rule. Make plain both the reward and penalties of this life."

I consider the pile of new clothing now lying atop the grand four-poster bed in my room. Uniforms, yes, but of the finest quality cloth. The quartermaster complained about my abnormally small size as if it were part of a grand conspiracy to make his tailoring difficult, even as he heaped rich burgundy tunics, wide matching sashes, and several fitted black pants on the counter before me.

More games. More rules. More symbols. From the grandeur of the Elders Council to the arbitrary challenges in the arena, and the ironclad hierarchy of the trainees.

"Don't listen to him, Lilac Girl." Tye grins at me, snatching me up and putting me back down on his lap. "The Citadel simply has more gold than it knows what to do

58

with, so it hires servants to embroider chairs—as if anyone's arse cares what manner of quilted flowers it's sitting on."

I smile. Try to smile. Try to ask about the trials too. But with Tye's pine-and-citrus scent caressing my body, his muscled thighs and arms wrapped securely around me, his nose gently nuzzling my ear, I suddenly find my eyelids too heavy to fight any longer.

Strong arms lift me from Tye's lap, the scent of rain surrounding me. Shade presses his lips to mine as he lowers me onto my soft bed, his dark hair falling around us. I open my mouth under his and kiss him back, eyes still closed, and I fall asleep to a warm, furry body pressed against mine, gentle wolf breaths fluttering over my neck.

THE FOLLOWING MORNING there is no time for nerves, with Kora appearing at dawn to inform River that the arena is ready for our first trial. I barely manage to pull on my uniform and accept a meat pie that River somehow acquired before discovering that the whole damn Citadel is heading to the same place we are.

"You won't be able to see the spectators from inside," Kora says, following my gaze to a cluster of no less than ten quints, who I swear are exchanging bets. "If that helps."

It doesn't.

"Stop gawking around and pay attention, mortal," Coal says, shouldering his way up to walk beside me, the large bowl-like structure beside the council tower growing larger with each step. "If you couldn't deign to stay awake long enough to hear the rules last night, you sure as hell are going to listen now."

I glance at Coal warily as Kora clears her throat and suddenly finds herself needed elsewhere.

"There are three trials," Coal says. "Quint, Individual, and Field, traditionally completed in that order—though this isn't strictly required. The quints may call for the trials at will, but each can be attempted no more than twice."

"What happens after two failures?" I ask, though my gut says I little want to know the answer.

"The quint dies," Coal says, tapping the runes on his neck and making me hate his honesty for a moment. "In the Quint Trial, two quints face off against each other to secure possession of the other's flag. The battle is over when a flag is retrieved or when one of the quint commanders sends up a surrender signal. The second trial is a one-on-one duel with another quint's warriors to test individual ability. And the final trial is outside the arena. Your quint is kidnapped and must reconnect and fight its way back to the Citadel."

"Brilliant," I say under my breath.

"You should have asked me to explain," Tye says, inviting himself to walk at my other shoulder. "I would have made it sound a lot better."

"Let's move," River calls, picking up the pace to a door at the base of the great bowl, which opens into a chamber that must be Coal's notion of paradise.

Weapons and armor fill the walls in neat rows, ordered by size and type. Little cubbies and clear glass drawers filled with everything from bandages to spare buckles rise to the ceiling. A wide wooden table sits in the middle, high enough to work standing up. A lower table in one corner has plenty of water for both drinking and washing, and there is a space in another corner outfitted with weights and practice dummies, in case someone needs a moment to warm up or channel nervous energy.

Shade paces around the room with flared nostrils, running his hands along the walls and benches.

"You aren't going to piss in the corners, are you?" I ask.

"Don't tempt me," Shade murmurs without a hint of humor, before turning to River. "I still dislike taking her in there."

"I don't see what choice we have," River says.

Shade growls and, as if obeying some instinct beyond his control, stops pacing and strides straight to me. His deep-red uniform shirt is rolled up, revealing corded forearms that go around me at once. Tucking my back against his body, the male buries his face in my neck, his deep breaths tickling my skin. His heart, right behind my ear, beats as quickly as my own.

I turn into Shade, resting my cheek against his muscled chest for a moment before rising onto my toes to link my arms around his neck.

Shade lifts me easily, moving one arm beneath my backside, the other coaxing my thighs until I wrap my legs obediently around his waist.

"It'll be okay, Shade," I whisper, hoping that he'll believe me even if I don't. "*I'll* be okay."

His hold only tightens in response, his face pressing deeper into my neck.

"Helpful as this is," Coal says, "if you keep it up, the mortal will be walking into the arena naked."

A wave of heat washes over Shade's skin as he sets me back on the floor, turning me reluctantly over to Coal's care.

Having laid out various pieces of leather armor that I assume somehow fit onto a body, Coal motions me to him. He takes one look at my befuddled expression and, with typical Coal efficiency, manhandles me into a loose stance, my arms raised slightly from my sides. His competent hands slide over my back, smoothing out my shirt before laying a piece of padded leather atop my shoulders, securing it in place. A trail of warmth stays on my skin long after his fingers leave, my body longing to lean into Coal's. I turn my head to look at Tye instead, waiting for the redhead to make one of his signature comments.

He doesn't. Tye's eyes, typically resting comfortably on my breasts or hips, are now drawn intently to my neck. A four-corded knot. Four, not five. I rub the skin. "You'd think a warrior quint would at least get something mildly ferocious for a rune," I say to Tye. "At this point, a mosquito would be an improvement."

"Are you listening?" Coal asks.

"When did you start talking?"

Growling, Coal grasps my hips and twists me around so he can tie the back laces of my new chest protector. His strong fingers move efficiently, tying the reinforced leather just tight enough that I can still breathe. "The entire trial will take place in the Light, so you need not worry about getting sucked into the Gloom during the fighting. Tye will carry our flag and draw the opponents' attention while

Shade and I go after the enemy flag. You'll stay with River. Once we have control of the flag, the trial ends."

"All right." I nod. "We win if we get control of the flag. How do we lose?"

"We don't. We're the most combat-ready quint on this mountain," Coal says. "But the three theoretical options are losing our flag, surrender, or death. The weapons are dulled, so the latter rarely happens in the first trial unless by the loser's pride. Losing is inevitable for one side or the other, but the humiliation of surrender is something else. Many, especially in the heat of the moment, stop thinking clearly."

"There are so many problems with this set-up, I don't even know where to begin," I say.

"Are you ready?" River asks, coming up beside me to check the buckles Coal just finished tightening. A wicked-looking sword is strapped down River's back. Though its edges are dulled in deference to the trial, the sheer weight and size of it would be enough to crack open a skull.

I put on as brave a face as I can muster. "Of course."

"You are a terrible liar." River crouches beside me— which, given how large he is, pretty much brings his face in line with mine. The uniform stretches tight over his muscled thighs and biceps, and I have to force my eyes away. The male's hands, calloused from weapons training, are warm against my cheeks. He holds my face in place so I can't look away, but I'd be helpless to look away anyway. His deep gray eyes and the smooth planes of his face are entrancing this close up. His scent washes over me as if on purpose, calming my frayed nerves. Each of them, in their own way, is doing his best to calm my nerves. "The most important thing in that arena is you, Leralynn. Not the bloody flag. We aren't going to set a record or show a third trial what three hundred years of field experience does for a quint. We are going to walk in there and come out safely. With you. Understand?"

I nod, the knot in my stomach easing slightly, but only until the sounding of a gong summons us to the arena sands.

9

LERA

I blink at the sun, which is brighter and hotter than it should be, the sand that spreads into a neat forever. With its smooth bowl-shaped sides, the three-hundred-foot arena has no clear demarcation of end and beginning, the wards designed to contain magic making it impossible to see beyond the sand's edges. The council is watching us from the upper rim of the arena, I know that much. The whole damn complement of the Citadel is likely watching. But from down here, it looks as though we're alone.

Us and the orange-clad quint filing in through the door on the far end. Malikai and his quint brothers. From this distance, I can't see their expressions, but I hope the prospect of facing Coal again is turning their bowels to mush. A bright orange flag, a sibling to the dark red one in

65

Tye's hands, wavers amidst the males in Malikai's quint as they affix it to the tallest warrior's arm.

A second gong sounds, and Klarissa's disembodied voice echoes over the arena. "The trial has begun."

Immediately, a wind picks up, raising a storm of sand to pelt our unprotected faces.

I lift an arm to shield myself, but a casual pulse of power from River has the sand suddenly bouncing off an invisible shield, the grains streaking back down to their yellow sea instead of filling my eyes. "Nice trick," I say, gazing around now that I can see again.

"The sand is about to get worse, if they are smart," River says, pointing into the distance, where the five males are gathering themselves together and advancing toward us like harbingers of doom. "The key for a new quint is to learn to combine their power."

I wait for the males around me to draw their weapons and become otherwise menacing, but the four seem totally at ease. I study their tall, lithe bodies and open faces, seeking the darkness that surely must lurk beneath their skin. I detect only calm. As if all this is little more than a dull but necessary wait before a meal.

The four of them are even chatting. No, not chatting. Bickering.

"It will be fine," Tye says, his green eyes glittering as he yanks the flag from Shade's hand. "It will be more than fine —it will be amusing."

"It will stop being amusing when you forget what the bloody hell you are supposed to be doing and decide to hump Malikai's leg."

"First, my tiger doesn't hump legs," Tye says, sounding offended. "I think you're confusing cats with *dogs*. And second, I don't need to remember what I'm doing once I shift—if your hands aren't growing out of your ass, you can tie the flag to me, and then all I need to do is run. Unless . . . Does my feline make you feel inadequate, Shade?"

I glance back toward Malikai's quint. They are a quarter of the way across the arena now and are, as River predicted, joining hands. My stomach tightens. "Children," I say, my voice pushing between Shade and Tye, "pay attention."

The words have just left my mouth when a new blast of air and sand pounds against us, the assault harsh enough to make me stumble. Wind whistles in my ears, echoing off the stone walls of the arena. I can hear the other quint shouting at each other, but not what they're saying.

River grabs on to my shoulder to keep me upright.

"Shouldn't we join as well?" I call over the sudden sandstorm.

"We aren't a new quint," River says calmly, extending his hand against the onslaught. The ground shifts slightly beneath one of the orange warriors.

The male stumbles. Falls. The quint disconnects and the attacking storm dies away.

"Tye will be fine," River says, plucking the flag from Tye's hand. "Go set up the flank. Once they are close enough, I'll release Tye with the flag. That will force them to scatter, and you can pick them apart to your heart's content. Try and keep the mess on the other side of the arena from Leralynn."

Coal and Shade, still in fae form, nod once and separate

right and left, jogging around the arena's sides as Malikai's regrouping quint continues to advance on us, their assault of wind and sand once again stressing River's shield.

"They want to pin us against the arena wall," River says casually, as if there isn't anything deadly about such a plan. From down here, the walls of the arena look like jagged yellow stones, giving off more preternatural heat than glowing embers. "We've greater experience in direct combat, so Malikai will try to keep his warriors from having to cross swords with any one of us."

River holds out his hand and the ground rumbles beneath Malikai's quint, though this time the males manage to keep their footing and the power of the wind pressing against us diminishes for only a moment. "It will be more difficult for me to hold them off when they are close, but at that point, there will no longer be a reason for them to approach us at all." He turns to Tye. "Ready? You bite me while I'm tying this on, and there will be hell to pay . . . eventually."

Tye grins widely and, in a flash of light, shifts into a gorgeous tiger with white-stuffed ears and sparkling green eyes. The tiger swings his wide muzzle to River and roars, opening its maw wide.

River swears and glances at the approaching quint, now halfway to us. "We don't have time for this, Tye. Stand down."

The tiger paws the sand and snarls, the feral predator taking over Tye's fae senses. But he is still there, my Tye. I can feel his essence, thriving and pulsing behind the teeth and snarls. He won't hurt me. I know it in my soul, even as my common sense protests. The tiger standing before us, ready to rip River into shreds, will not harm me.

I pluck the flag from River's hand before the quint commander can argue and hold my palm out to Tye, catching his green eyes with my own. "I'll do it," I say, my voice soft. "Stand back, River."

The tiger's nostrils flare delicately, his long tongue lapping at his nose. I take a step toward him and crouch, my palm still out despite River's warning growl.

The tiger yawns. Then condescends to step forward. My heart quickens, those sharp, white teeth glistening in the sun.

"Good boy," I whisper, fear and trust colliding inside my chest. "It's me, Tye. It's you and me."

Another step. His large orange head comes in line with my face, the powerful jaws strong enough to sever my jugular in a single snap. I stay still even so, waiting. Not breathing. A final step and the tiger's head reaches me. Lowers.

And rubs against my shoulder with enough force to knock me flat on my butt.

"Very funny, kitty." Climbing back onto my feet, I tie the flag around the tiger's neck like a bright neckerchief, while the animal stands still but for his tail, which swishes back and forth like a pendulum. I test the knot and glance at River, who watches the exchange with a mix of rapt attention and amusement.

"Good." Taking my hand in his, River pulls me away from Tye, whose tiger launches across the arena, his wide paws kicking up sand.

Someone in Malikai's quint shouts, pointing to the tiger and flag, which streams like a scarf from the animal's neck. The quint pauses. There is but a quarter of the arena separating them from us now, with Coal and Shade waiting far at their backs and Tye now going on a merry dance across the sand.

River pulls me close to him. "The hard part is over," he says, his grip reassuring. "You and I are of no more value to them."

I nod, waiting for the five warriors to turn back toward the flag and the greater threat that Coal and Shade pose.

Two against five are not odds I like, but River's sheer confidence in his quint brothers flows through his skin into mine. I wonder how many battles it took to forge that measured calm that he projects—as if even now, in the midst of a trial, we've all the time in the world to get it right.

Two of Malikai's warriors separate, their attention going to Shade and Coal. The sand flies from beneath their boots as they retrace the very ground they just conquered.

Coal and Shade wait, luring their adversaries to the other side of the arena as ordered. Coal's opponent reaches him first, and I wince for the orange-clad male as Coal's blade strikes his ribs, dulled metal flashing in the sunlight.

The male drops to his knees with a scream, the fire he'd been kindling dying in his palms.

On the other side, Shade flashes into his wolf, the beast's snarl a battle cry of its own.

"Go!" Malikai shouts, and the three remaining fae—the ones who are supposed to be going after Tye and our flag—rush at River and me instead.

My heart stops before leaping into a gallop. "They don't want the flag, do they?" I say, even as I feel River's power pulsing through him, his free arm drawing his sword. "They are going after *me*."

River pushes me behind him, his broad back covering me from the assault of wind and sand and steel. "Yes," he says calmly, his voice rumbling through my body, purpose radiating off him as fiercely as the heat blazing from the arena's walls.

I swallow, my world narrowing for a moment on my quint commander. The dark hair at the nape of his neck is damp with sweat. His pulse, beating evenly beneath the three runes that he accepted for my sake. His back, swelling with each slow breath, undaunted by the murder riding at us full force.

The moment ends and I tear my gaze back to the arena. The three warriors are only ten yards away now. The first trial isn't supposed to end in death, but those standards are based on immortal bodies, not fragile human flesh. The fae's blades might be dulled, but their magic isn't. What would be a survivable wound for fae would kill me outright. And the gleam in Malikai's eyes says he knows it.

Is counting on it.

My palms dampen with sweat.

Three fae warriors against one.

Except I'm not blind. Not deaf. I can see the fury in the males' eyes, feel the power of River's magic slide. I reach for my dagger, the small weapon Coal insisted I carry. The blade is so insignificant that Malikai—now just a few paces

71

away—laughs, the harsh sound vibrating through me. My body begs me to defend it.

Something inside me rises to answer the plea, the sensation so native that I know the *something* inside me is mine—and yet I'm just as certain that I've never felt it before. Don't even know what *it* is.

The sand and wind pelt my face, and I bite my lip to keep from begging River to strengthen the shield. He is moving forward now, shifting to offense, and he needs that shield flexible to mount his own assault.

My heart pounds at being left alone. Even as River's blade becomes a whirlwind between me and Malikai, as Coal and Shade rush to our aid, their respective sword and teeth already pointed and ready to strike. Even as I trust the males to protect me, my need to protect myself roars.

The *something* inside me pulses in answer. Grows hot. Shoves against its tether and demands release. I recognize the sensation now—it's like what happened in the Gloom, when the quint connected and the magic pulled through me.

Malikai takes one more step. He's close enough that one lucky lunge past River's blade will have him at my throat. His pale eyes gleam in the harsh sunlight, his tan face pulled back in a victory grimace.

The terror inside me snaps the tether blindly, and the ground beneath us explodes in a column of sand and rock. Relief floods my body, making every nerve stand on end.

River spins, his eyes meeting mine with a flash of the one thing I've yet to see in the commander—*panic*. With the next breath, he turns back toward the shaken attackers, who are already reclaiming their blades. River's arms come out before him, as if it were he, not I, who just made the earth tremble. "We surrender!" he bellows to the sky, his voice echoing through the arena. "Stop the trial. Now."

The air around us thickens at once, holding everyone in place to stop the fight.

10

LERA

$\mathcal{M}$y world roars around me, the exploding earth and River's bellow of surrender ringing in my ears as the males herd me from the arena into the preparation room that we left a short eternity ago. The well of power I felt pulsing inside me is nothing but a phantom memory now, so nonexistent that I wonder if it wasn't River who exposed the earth after all.

A fine tremble vibrates my body. Malikai and his quint wanted to kill me. Would have killed me. *Stars.*

River, who has yet to release my arm, now pulls me in front of him, running his hands up my arms and shoulders and neck until coming to rest on my cheeks. His broad, rough palms cupping my face, River peers into my eyes with an intensity that robs my breath, searching for something.

Answers, probably. Ones that I don't have.

74

The raw emotion, a mix of fear and awe and something I can't identify, turns the warrior's face from beautiful to stunning. The rarity of seeing anything but command in River's features—now twice in only minutes—makes my heart falter.

"What the hell happened out there?" Tye asks, his green eyes still tinged with a feral freedom. His chest heaves, his fiery hair falling in sweat-soaked locks over his face as he paces in front of us. No, not paces—circles. Chasing a nonexistent tail. "What did I miss?"

"A soon-to-be-dead third trial named Malikai went after our mortal." Coal's voice is low and cold, absent of emotion. Mimi once told me to fear a quiet dog over a growling one, because the former has already decided to attack and feels no need to warn you off. Watching Coal now, I understand what she meant. Coal crosses his arms, his dark eyes boring into River. "But that little explains the surrender, River. The bastards would have all been dead long before laying a finger on Lera. You know that."

"Yes, but Leralynn didn't." River rubs his face, his confident expression faltering for a weary moment. "Your *mortal*, Coal, discovered she had magic and took her safety into her own hands. I thought it best we not let the whole damn Citadel know about it."

For the first time since walking from the arena, I find my voice. "I . . . It wasn't on purpose. I don't even know what I did."

"You wielded magic, Leralynn." River turns to face me again. "Earth magic. Same as what I have an affinity for, fortunately. It all happened so quickly that I'm confident the burst, crude as it was, will be dismissed as mine."

Shade comes up behind me as he did before the trial, oozing need and possession as he wraps a muscled arm around my waist, his other hand resting just above my elbow. Shade's breath on my hair is warm and quick. He nuzzles his nose into the space behind my ear, his hair brushing my collarbone. The cocoon of safety envelops me at once, and it's all I can do not to close my eyes and sink into the male's hard shoulder, letting myself imagine that nothing but his earthy scent fills the world.

"I'm all right," I murmur to the male behind me.

"I'm not," Shade answers, inhaling my scent, his hold tightening.

Tye stops his turning and drapes himself across a chair instead, one leg hooked over the armrest. "And why, might I inquire, do we not want the whole damn Citadel to know about Lilac Girl's power? I, for one, am looking forward to seeing the look on Klarissa's face when she finds out."

"Because of the Individual Trial," Coal says, nodding his understanding to River. "We suffer a bit of humiliation now for the sake of preserving the mortal's element of surprise for the one-on-one test. Which also means that we must either delay retaking the Quint Trial until after the Individual, or somehow ensure that Lera can manage to *not* come to our rescue next time."

A knock halts our conversation. Well, the males' conversation, as I'm still unsure what all this means, much less what to say about it.

"I'll get it," I say, extricating myself from Shade's hold to open the door—onto a very befuddled Kora. She's in uniform, the emerald shade of her belted tunic picking up the gem in her ear. Her blue eyes are as wide as mine must be.

Running a hand through her short hair, as she seems to have been doing for a while now, the female looks around the room, shifting her weight uncomfortably. "I . . ."

"I imagine there is some discussion taking place beyond these walls," River says, his voice collected as he rises to his feet and bows, his hands clasped loosely behind his back. A transformation from deadly warrior to well-mannered prince, all in the space of a blink.

"Everyone saw you winning," Kora says bluntly. "The whole bloody Citadel came to watch you destroy Malikai. You could have wiped the sand with them, even when the bastards went after Lera. And then, a few heartbeats before your victory would have been undeniable, you . . . surrendered." Kora stops speaking, the silence its own question.

No one answers it.

Kora lowers her face.

"What conclusion do you draw from all this, Kora?" River asks.

The female meets River's eyes. "That you made a decision for reasons other than fearing for your lives. And that you will be paying a high enough price for it as is, without being asked to satisfy my curiosity on top of that."

A corner of River's mouth twitches and he offers

another small bow to our guide, while my own heart pounds. "And now you are here because we are still first trials and are thus expected somewhere."

She nods reluctantly. "Breakfast."

"And if we're not hungry?"

"Quints are now expected to spend at least two meals a day at the mess hall—"

"So the council can keep a leash on our schedules," River finishes with a sigh. "And let me guess, Klarissa recommends that we start now."

THE LOW DIN of the mess hall goes silent the instant the five of us step inside, our uniforms still soaked with sweat and sand. The long room is stunning, like the rest of the Citadel. Tall windows on three sides let in streams of sunlight, and thick oak rafters brace a peaked ceiling, giving the whole space a rustic charm. The walls are hung with colorful silk tapestries, the largest of which depicts a beautiful female with clouds of brunette curls and a harp so real, I can almost hear the ethereal music.

River's back is straight, calm dominance radiating from every inch of his body. If I feel like a disgraced insect walking onto a stage, the prince of Slait is striding into a throne room and heading straight for the meat table.

As we walk to the food, I'm relieved to hear the voices slowly start back up.

My mouth waters in spite of itself. Thanks to Shade's hunting, we ate well during our journey here, but the

Citadel mess hall must rival that of a palace. Thick slices of juicy venison, rabbit quarters, a whole crispy pig with an apple baked into its mouth. A separate table holds plates of fruit and cheese, the fresh aromas dancing with the smoky scent of meat. "Do I just—"

River, whose plate is already filling, turns and hands the whole thing to me. "You can take whatever you like."

"You don't mind if I cut in, do you?" Malikai's poisonous voice interjects, and I feel River's body stiffen for the smallest of heartbeats before his large hand settles on my waist.

"Not at all, sir," the prince tells the third trial, with such impeccable courtesy that I feel a shiver run down my spine. "We'll return once you've made your selection." Hand still on me, River guides me to a table where the others are already sitting, their plates nonexistent. River pulls a chair out for me and nods toward the food. "Eat, Leralynn. Malikai and his ilk will be sure to need all the food tables until the meal is over. It's a common way in which third trials try to torment their juniors."

I survey the calm faces around me. "You knew this would happen," I say, nodding at the empty tabletop. "You didn't even bother getting plates."

Shade stretches, his lithe body lazily claiming the space around me and all the air from my lungs. "Do you imagine any of us will go hungry, cub?" he asks with a grin. "The runes may keep me from leaving the Citadel grounds, but they don't stop game from coming in."

My stomach growls, the scent of hot food so tempting, I

all but shake with want. "We'll wait until you hunt, then." I push the plate away.

River pushes it right back. "Eat. I, for one, am looking forward to a fresh kill. Plus"—his voice lowers—"we can't leave until someone eats. So either you dine like a smart being, or we'll be reduced to grabbing scraps with our hands once the plates are cleared."

The males keep up a steady stream of conversation, sprawling in their chairs as if every fae warrior in the room isn't watching them. As if they're here by choice and have graciously permitted the others to share our space. Shade drapes an arm over the back of my chair, fingers playing idly with the tip of my braid, sending shivers through me. Given the force with which Malikai is stabbing his food, I imagine the display looks as convincing to others as it would to me if I weren't sitting close enough to Coal to see his white-knuckled fists.

It's all for me, I realize. The males' willingness to endure humiliations that should be hundreds of years behind them. To drop to their knees on the hard council floor and accept runes that trap them in a place they despise. My throat constricts, a sense of belonging, of fierce connection, filling my soul. I don't know how I can ever repay the four warriors for the gift, but I will try.

River ensures that we are the last ones to leave the dining hall, chatting jovially until even Malikai gives up waiting for us to slink away.

That done, we take another long walk around the grounds before Coal growls that I'll forget what little riding I've learned and takes me to the stables, where Czar and

Sprite meet us with whickering welcomes. Riding turns into a long sparring lesson in a sunlit glen behind the dormitories.

Another gift, the training and the resulting fatigue. The one sort of balm that Coal can offer my fraying nerves. It almost works too. Almost.

The sun has set by the time we return to the suite. I smile weakly at the males, whatever borrowed strength that fueled me through the day choosing this very moment to depart my body.

"I'm going to bed," I declare, not waiting for a response, ignoring the sharp cut of River's eyes, the tick in Coal's jaw, and Tye half rising to stop me as I walk back to my room. The moment I'm inside, I turn to shut the door at once, staying with my forehead pressed against the thick wood.

It takes me three slow breaths to find enough strength to reach up and engage the latch. Once I do, I slide down to my knees, my palms rasping against the finely carved wood. Tears I didn't know were flooding my eyes now spill down my cheeks, my body trembling like a frightened rabbit's. I'm tired. I'm scared. And I'm so damn confused that I can't think straight. Some bloody quint warrior I am.

My fingers trace the runes on my neck, as they have over and over since the damn marks were burned into my skin. Four cords. Not five. Because one of us doesn't belong here, no matter how brave a face the males put on, how much they pretend that having to repeat their Citadel initiation for my sake is no great burden. That today's surrender, spurred into existence by nothing other than my fear, is naught but a small inconvenience.

I'm mortal, not stupid. I can see through their facade as easily as they can create it.

Scrubbing my sleeve across my face, I sniffle as softly as I can and turn toward my bed—only to stumble back toward the door as a sudden light flashes atop my covers.

Shade.

I glower at the wolf curled against my pillow, its nose tucked piously under its tail. He's been here all along, watching me break to pieces and then shifting before I could make him explain the damn intrusion. "Get out," I say quietly. "Or I will. And don't pretend you can't understand me. You bloody *smell* my meaning."

Nothing.

"Fine." I turn, reaching for the latch. My hand is halfway there when the light flashes again and a guilty-looking male replaces the giant gray wolf on my bed. "I didn't mean to intrude," Shade says sheepishly, swinging his legs over the side of the mattress to brace powerful forearms on his knees. Dressed only in the black uniform pants, which mold around his waist, thighs, and more, Shade is his usual shirtless self. Powerful muscles bunch under smooth, tan skin as he flexes his fingers. His golden eyes flick to mine, then to the floor. "By the time I realized you wished to be alone, it was a little late to announce myself."

I wrap my arms around my ribcage, my back against the door. "If the next words out of your mouth are 'what's wrong'—"

"I was rather planning on keeping my mouth shut." Shade rises from the bed and walks slowly toward me, extending a hand that stops just short of brushing my shoulder. Even after the long day, his body is lithe and deadly, each flick of muscle an economy of lupine motion. His yellow eyes brush my body hungrily, sending a reflexive jolt of fire through my core. My hands long to touch him, even as I want to shove him out the window.

Shade's nostrils flare delicately against my neck. "You are freezing, cub."

"No, I'm not." I rub my arms. Now that he's said it, though, I realize Shade is right. I am cold. A bone-deep weary chill of stress and fatigue that no amount of blankets could conquer. The fact that the male knew it before I did sends another jolt of heat through me. "I mean, it's nothing a bit of sleep won't cure."

Shade moves closer—which I would have thought impossible—until he's bracing his hands on the door on either side of my head. His broad frame fills my world, his dark hair and yellow eyes forming a cocoon. The moonlight coming through my window silhouettes the hard cut of his hips. "I have a better idea." His whisper brushes my cheek, his wolfish scent and my own rebelliously growing need trapping me as securely as any rope.

Shade's soft lips graze the corner of my mouth and trail up my neck, leaving tiny burning footprints all the way to my ear. "Trust me?"

I can't answer. Can't speak, for fear of him pulling away from me. My self-control is worn too threadbare for such heroics.

Shade's arms slide over my body, hooking beneath my knees and shoulder blades. My breath catches in my throat as the male lifts me against his chest and strides smoothly to the window, its curtains pulled back to welcome the star-filled sky. Opening the latch with one practiced motion, Shade vaults over the sill and onto the damp grass below. Even with me in his arms, Shade lands softly on the balls of his feet and carries me off into the darkness.

SHADE

*S*hade hadn't meant to intrude on Lera. He truly hadn't. By the time he realized he *was*, it was too late. Moving easily through the night, he pressed her to his chest. The cold air brushing his skin was startling against the girl's warmth, the combination alone rousing his senses.

Shade knew he was playing with fire. With the same delicious, loin-gripping, soul-consuming flames that had guided him free of a decade in wolf form and now challenged him to live every moment of the now. And therein lay the problem.

Shade had known he was in love with Lera since he first shifted form, but the wolf part of him, it wasn't one for subtle. Not when it *wanted*. And certainly not when it *claimed*. Which it was a breath away from doing, whether or not Shade's higher senses gave permission.

If the wolf had had its way, Shade would have claimed

Lera nearly two weeks ago. And then proceeded to tear apart anyone and anything that got too close to his newly claimed mate. It was an instinct poorly conducive to a healthy quint, and it wasn't one that Lera would likely tolerate, not with that streak of bravery and independence of hers that made Shade's breath catch on a regular basis.

The other males knew, of course—smelled how close to mating his wolf was becoming—and each in his own way had warned Shade to mind his animal or keep the bloody hell away from the girl. Since the latter was impossible, it would have to be the former. No matter how trying the night was likely to become.

Lera's eyes were drooping closed as she entrusted Shade with her body like he'd asked. He lowered his nose to her hair, inhaling the way her lilac scent mixed with the crisp night air one more time, before opening the heavy door leading down, down, down a spiral staircase. The slight taste of sulfur filled Shade's mouth at once, along with a damp kind of chill. The candlelit air grew thicker as they descended, an odd fog haunting the passage.

Lera opened her eyes, blinking in delicious wonder as the sound of rushing water echoed from the stony depths, growing louder with each step. A final turn, and the spiral staircase yielded to a vast cavern—one of the Citadel's priceless treasures.

Thousands of candles, each as unique as the rocky shelf it stood on, burned with flames that consumed none of the delicate wax. The flickering lights reflected in the half dozen pools of water, some still and others bubbling, that made up the cave's underground springs. "Welcome to the bathhouse," Shade said softly.

"Bathhouse? That word is woefully inadequate." Lera's velvety brown eyes sparkled as she looked around. The magic of watching her see the cavern's springs and geysers for the first time was already making the excursion worth it. That was one of the human's most irresistible charms—everything was new and rich and exciting. It was as if Shade could live every wonder of life all over again through Lera. She cleared her throat. "Where are the . . . bathers?"

"At this hour, I imagine they are sleeping," Shade said. The cavern was seldom used in the evening, save for visiting fae, as it was more practical for the trainees to attend to bathing earlier in the day. It was the reason he'd brought Lera here, to offer her an oasis of private calm after two days of being watched and assaulted and discussed and tested.

Lera stirred in Shade's arms, her feet seeking the ground, as Shade maneuvered to the far pool. It was his favorite, perfectly hot and deep, with slightly murky bubbling water. The girl's motion rubbed over Shade's already taut cock, sending a jolt of fire through his loins. The male swallowed a curse and nipped the girl's ear.

"You've done more than enough the past two days, cub. Let me take it from here. You can stand up to the Elders Council, face an arena trial, and discover magic again tomorrow, if you wish." Still supporting the backs of Lera's knees, Shade set her down on the pool's smooth stone lip. The warm tub was smaller than the other pools in the cavern, but still large enough to let several fae soak comfortably, and the soft foam of its bubbling waters lapped the stone.

Shade's heart quickened as he crouched beside Lera, pulling off her leather boots and undoing her long braid. Shade hadn't the power to halt the Citadel's trials, but a massage and a warm bath, yes, that much he could give the girl.

That much and no more. That was the rub of it.

A soft moan escaped Lera's lips as Shade ran his fingers through her thick, silky hair, the tiny sound going mercilessly to his cock. His body tightened, his hands stilling on Lera's scalp while he swallowed and fought for breath that suddenly came at a premium.

"Are you all right?" Lera asked, shifting until her eyes met his, sending another jolt of need through Shade's core.

No. No, he wasn't all right. He was one breath away from pouncing. Shade shook himself—only to find Lera's palms on either side of his face, her lips so close to his skin that he could feel their heat. In the flickering candlelight, Lera's melted-chocolate eyes were as deep and warm as the cavern itself.

Shade's heart stuttered a beat then pounded so hard that the impact against his head and cock drowned out the world.

"Shade, what is it?" Lera's hands slid from his cheeks to the tops of his shoulders, each friction of flesh spurring his desire.

Shade shuddered again, this time more violently, and caught Lera's wrist. "It would be better if you just enjoyed, cub," he said hoarsely. "I won't be able to keep myself in check if you start . . . reciprocating."

Lera frowned, tipping her head to the side so a single strand of hair fell over her dusting of freckles. "Do you have to?" she asked slowly, though Shade could see the rapid *lub dub, lub dub* of her pulse in the hollow of her neck. "Keep yourself in check?"

Stars. "Yes," Shade said firmly. "I very much do."

Her shoulders fell, a hint of pain flashing in her eyes almost too quickly to catch.

Shade's heart tightened. "It isn't because I don't want you, cub. On the contrary. I want you too greatly."

"Then let me explore you." Lera rose to her knees, her voice filled with power. "When is it my turn? I want to touch you, discover what makes you—"

"There is very little secret as to what makes me hard, Lera. You sitting beside me is enough to drive me insane. But tonight isn't about me. It's about you."

A quick flash of her brow. "Then I should have a say in how it proceeds."

Shade caught Lera's free hand before it could reach its pulsing target, and pulled both of her slender wrists into one hold. The night was quickly heading where it should not, and Shade's sweat had little to do with the steaming bath. "I'll make you a bargain, cub," he said, his breath hitching. "You keep your hands to yourself and I'll make it worth your while tonight."

Lera's eyes glazed over slightly, her thighs tensing.

Holding her gaze, Shade released Lera's wrists and pulled loose the laces of her shirt collar and that wide sash holding the tunic against the girl's slim waist. He moved slowly, savoring every touch as if life, not cloth, hung in the balance. Shirt loosened, he pulled it over Lera's head in one short motion, brushing his hands down her sides as soon as they were bare.

She was new to this, though Shade had no idea how that was possible unless all the males in the mortal world were bloody blind. Still, the girl seemed unaware of her distracting beauty, and while she plainly enjoyed touch, she was shy about her own pleasure.

Lera's breath caught as he removed her chest bind, her face heating as the round swells of her breasts tumbled free. Lera's nipples, pink and all but begging for Shade's mouth, stiffened with their sudden taste of air. Shade brushed his hands down Lera's supple skin, tracing his fingers along her collarbone, her sides, her hips, his gaze drinking in her face. She bit her lip, her eyes drifting closed. Even out of his wolf form, Shade scented the mix of desire and hesitation that hung around her, thick as perfume. The pants could wait until they were in the tub.

Making short work of his own boots, Shade lifted Lera against his chest and walked them both into the bubbling pool. The water—so hot, it rose in steamy curls into the air—soaked at once through Shade's pants. Setting Lera on the cleverly molded bench beneath the water's surface, he let the bubbles shroud her body while he tugged away her bottoms. "It's a bath, cub," he said into her ear. "It's not generally taken dressed in Lunos."

Lera's eyes narrowed. Pushing away from the bench, she slid toward him, straddling his bent knee. The soft feel of her sex along his cloth-covered thigh, her skin pressing against his, her hands—

Shade growled, the tremor running through his cock and muscles. If the girl didn't stop squirming and let him make her scream his way, the evening was not going to end well at all.

"Let's make tonight about us," Lera said, her hands now on his pectorals. His nipples.

"No." Lifting Lera, he stood the girl up, turning her safely sideways. With one arm around her waist, keeping her that way, Shade used his other hand to open Lera's thighs and stroke his fingers firmly along her slit, back and forth, back and forth, until she clenched with need. "I told you I would make it worth your while," he purred into her ear, his hand halting its progression. "Now, will you behave if I let you go?"

She gasped, wriggling against his hold, her sex seeking the pressure of his fingers again.

"Will you behave?" Shade bit softly along Lera's neck in emphasis. In possession. The girl gasped softly at each new nip, her sex growing slicker despite the water, her weight shifting desperately in his hold. He circled her opening, felt it clenching with desire, and knew—savored knowing—that he could make her scream in frustration in a heartbeat just by moving away, only to bring her to the verge of release again with a scrape of a nail along her swollen nub. The wolf inside Shade stirred. "Will you behave?" he demanded again, moving his fingers in a slow, torturous circle that closed in on her apex.

Lera's fingernails raked his shoulder. "Stop talking, Shade."

"No jumping on me," he ordered, punctuating the rule with a flick of his fingers against her pulsing sex. "No wandering hands. And no testing my control over my instincts." He pressed his lips to her ear. "I promise you, there is very little left to test there just now."

She nodded quickly, likely ready to agree to just about anything to make his hand move again. "Not. Fair."

Shade chuckled, his cock pulsing as he held her there, riding that knife's edge once more before loosening his hold.

He should have known better.

He truly should have, considering that the girl he was holding had stood up to the Elders Council of the Citadel only yesterday. Lera was no cub. And she didn't take well to orders.

Shade's eyes widened as Lera seized the moment his arm loosened to twist around and leap, wrapping her legs around his waist. Shade's arms gripped her backside reflexively to keep them both from toppling over in the waist-high pool. His mouth opened in a startled protest, but she was ready for that too. Opening her lips, Lera claimed Shade's mouth with hers until his cock throbbed painfully against his too-tight breeches, and all thought narrowed to a screaming, fiery need. Until it was *him* ready to whimper and beg.

Stars.

One moment, Shade was certain he'd had her as taut as a violin string, his hand rushing through her blazing sex at his will.

And then, as fast as a bloody viper, she'd reversed it all.

Lera's hands tangled in his hair, her legs wrapping around his bare waist, her breasts full and so close to his mouth that he'd have taken her nipple between his lips if only they weren't currently occupied with hers. Whatever thoughts Shade's mind had still managed to hang on to exploded to shreds that little cared for anything but what was before him. *Who* was before him.

His mate.

LERA

 $\mathcal{M}$ y body blazes as I wrap my legs around Shade's hard waist, my hands twining through his thick black hair. His soft lips and hard hands claim me, my tongue tracing his dangerously elongated canines, my heart pounding against my ribs. The water's slightly sulfurous taste tangles with Shade's earthy scent, drowning out the world.

Shade's calloused hands cup my backside, strong fingers digging into my skin. I can feel him, his hardness bulging against his breeches and pressing against my aching sex. He did this, kindled this flame that now consumes me. This mind-churning need that glazes over my eyes, these jolts of desire that make my thighs quiver, this abyss of frustration. My fingers curl against Shade's shoulder, my fingernails digging mercilessly into his flesh.

Mine, my body screams. My male. My fire. My time to take.

The only sounds are harsh breathing and trickling water.

It drips from our bare skin, the moist air tickling my face, my neck, the tops of my aching breasts, as Shade walks us to the edge of the pool, never taking his mouth off mine. His pants are heavy with wetness, and I shove my heel into the waistband as he sets me on the pool's lip, laying my discarded shirt down to soften the smooth stone.

Unwrapping one hand from Shade's neck, I reach for his hardness, bearing it so roughly that he growls against my mouth. Stars, Shade is large. Hard and wide and so long, I can little understand how the male can even wear pants. The vibrations in his chest race through me, alerting each nerve to the male's claim. My breath quickens in response, blood rushing to my thighs, my core, my sex.

I bite his lip, rejoicing in his sudden wakeful jolt.

Gripping my sides, Shade shoves my back onto the stone while he remains standing in the bubbling pool. I tighten my legs around his waist, greedily watching water slither down his heaving chest, the grooves of his muscled abdomen, the narrow cut of his hips. He kicks his pants away. His cock rises hungrily, so tan and velvety smooth that a small moan of impatience escapes my throat. His beautiful face is intense with focus, its angles looking carved out of warm stone in the candlelight, his golden eyes glowing. My backside tightens, pressing harder against him as his hard cock brushes my dripping slit.

Shade's eyes flash, his nostrils flaring with a feral intent that sends another bolt of lightning through me. Bracing his forearms against my knees, Shade breaks my legs' hold on his waist with one strong pump of his hands and holds my tingling thighs open before him.

The sudden rush of air against my swollen sex is an agony of deprivation, and my body roars, already feeling his phantom fullness. I buck.

Shade bares his teeth. His eyes narrow on my slick opening, the tip of his tongue brushing his teeth hungrily. He pushes my thighs wider, making it impossible to so much as clench the aching lips of my sex. I writhe, my hands and heels digging into the stone, my hips bucking as my body seeks a way to reclaim its grip on his.

I don't see Shade's hand move until I feel a sharp slap against my raised backside, the crack of his palm against my wet flesh echoing through the chamber. I cry out as prickles of fire explode over my skin, spider-webbing through my flesh. Before I can close my thighs, Shade has my legs up on his shoulders, his hand rubbing away the lingering sting. The heat radiating from the male makes the hot spring seem chill in comparison.

Shade's fingers run the length of my slit, the slick, steady pressure making me moan. The fingers stop.

So does my breath.

Locking his eyes on mine, Shade plunges one finger inside me and rotates it leisurely. My eyes widen.

"You," I demand through gritted teeth. "I want you. All of you, damn it."

Shade's teeth flash, and he leans down, his tongue flickering mercilessly against my bud. Once, twice, *stars*.

Each tiny lap of his tongue shoves me an inch closer to the edge of an abyss. His teeth graze the spot his tongue just visited, and I shout, my voice echoing through the chamber.

"Tight," Shade growls, lifting his head as a second finger enters me. A third. Pulling out, Shade spreads open my sex, positioning his dripping cock at my opening. His eyes grip mine.

My heart speeds in anticipation. An intoxicating mix of fear and need seizes my lungs. I try to grip the stone with slick hands. It will hurt. I know it will. The first time with a man always does, and the sheer size of Shade seems impossible to accept.

"Lera." My name on Shade's lips has me pressing into him without thought.

He thrusts, the length of him filling me, striking deep inside.

I gasp at the perfect fullness, even as a ripple of pain pierces my flesh.

Shade stills, his hands suddenly cupping my face, his eyes blazing with a feverish need. He pants but stays motionless. "Did I hurt you, cub?"

"No. Yes." I shudder. Shade's hardness inside me fills an emptiness I never knew existed even as it stretches my tender flesh. "I . . ."

His eyes widen, their golden irises flashing in the dim candlelight. "It is your first time," he whispers. "Stars."

"Don't stop," I say.

"Never." He rises above me, one hand gripping my backside and lifting me off the stone, his other hand finding my apex and rubbing in a way that chases the soreness into a pulsing need. Pleasure washes over me in slowly growing waves until I ride up against Shade again, urging him back into motion.

His eyes glaze over, his nostrils flaring as he pulls back just enough to thrust obligingly, the great length of him sliding along my slickness. He thrusts again. Again. Harder. Faster. His cock pounding, the wet slap of flesh against flesh echoing through the cavern. His thumb flicks against my bud until I'm panting and moaning so loud, I can't catch my breath.

Each slam of him ripples through me, each vibration more powerful than the last. His fingers move quickly along my sex at the same time, building my pleasure until I shout. Beg. "Shade . . ." Just saying his name is a struggle. "Please. Shade!"

"Wait for it," he pants. "Soon."

"I can't," I whimper, waves of pleasure cascading through my core, hot and gripping, tingling down the length of my slick thighs.

"Almost." He pulses inside me, his cock fuller and harder than moments ago. "Come for me, Lera," he commands, his thumb skimming across my nub one final time. "Come now."

Pent-up sensations crash through me like an avalanche, my body tightening in a glorious agony that has me shouting Shade's name as he shouts mine, his thick warmth spilling into my belly. Gasping, I feel my backside collapse back down onto the shirt-covered stone, echoes of energy still rippling through my body.

"Cub." Shade breathes harshly as he wraps his arms

around me, lowering me back into the tub to cradle me against him. His hands run over my back and thighs. I rest my head on his hard chest, listening to his heart pounding in rhythm with mine, our breath and hearts the only sounds for a long moment.

"Are you very sore?" he asks quietly.

I nuzzle my cheek against his warm skin. "It was exquisitely worth it."

He places his palm just below my abdomen and a magic as soft as a spider's silk caresses me, sinking into my body with a soothing sigh. "Better? You need not worry about offspring with a fae and human. There is that too."

"There are undeniable advantages to having a knowledgeable and experienced healer wolf around." I grin up at him, frowning as I catch his jaw tensing at my words.

"There are disadvantages to having one of those around too," Shade whispers, suddenly avoiding my eyes.

"Like what?"

"We'll discover soon enough, I'm sure." He rubs his hand over his face. "Whatever stupid things I do in the next while, just know that I'm sorry."

13

LERA

I wake to a pleasant soreness, rays of sunlight pricking my eyes. The white sheets of my soft four-poster bed are cool against my cheek, and small puffs of warm, wolfish breath tickle the back of my neck. Last night's adventures are a warm haze in my core, and I little remember getting back from the baths. As for what we did in that hot spring . . . My body tingles in memory of last night, the corners of my mouth tugging up as I reach to brush the wolf's fur.

"You know what's nice about this morning, lass?" Tye drawls from the doorway. Letting himself into my bedchamber, he strides casually to the very same windowsill that Shade vaulted over in yesterday's escape and perches himself atop it. Tye's long fingers interlace behind his head, his biceps bulging under a thin white undershirt. His red hair is mussed, his silver earring glinting in the sunlight.

100

"What?" I say warily.

"That someone is in deep trouble, and for once, it's not me."

I sit up in bed, tugging the blanket to cover my bare chest and crossing my arms. Shade, damn him, wisely stays in wolf form. It's an effort of will to remind myself that Tye can't read my thoughts. Or my memories. "Have you heard of knocking?"

The smile on Tye's lips widens, his nostrils flaring delicately. "The door is beside the point." He drops his voice. "I can smell *it* on you from out there, Lilac Girl. We all can."

Flames consume my face, mixing together with a stomach-clenching guilt. My gaze darts around in search of a dark hole to hide in and comes up empty. I stick my chin into the air, in hopes that my mind will catch up with my show of confidence. I asked Tye to bed me after the piranha battle, and he—the male who thinks a bed filled with any fewer than two beings is a criminal waste of space—declined, wanting the whole quint present for our first joining.

Things didn't turn out that way, clearly.

"Fine. You smell *it*." I swallow, making myself meet Tye's gaze. "My bedding decisions are not a democratic process. And are, therefore, none of your bloody business."

"What, none *at all* of my business?" Tye purrs, the glint in his green eyes growing even brighter. "That could be up for debate, though perhaps not this very morning. At any rate, I didn't really come here to watch you squirm, lass. I came to watch that flea-bitten stray squirm. And to tell him that if he thinks remaining in wolf form is going to save him from River's wrath, he is very much mistaken."

"I repeat," I say, my voice firmer. "My bedding decisions are—"

"It isn't your bedding decisions that anyone is questioning." Tye's voice drops its humor. "It's Shade's. And no, he doesn't get to make certain choices alone." Hopping down from the windowsill, Tye strides toward the bed and addresses the wolf directly. "Friendly advice, Shade. Get the hell out of here before River decides he's not going to wait until Lera awakens, and comes in here himself."

I frown.

A flash of light has Shade sitting in my bed, his broad shoulders shifting with a heavy sigh. "Thank you, Tye." His eyes dart to me for a moment before finding the floor. "But unlike fine wine, River's temper isn't going to improve with time. I might as well get it over with now."

Tye winces. "I wouldn't want to be in your place."

Wrapping a sheet around myself, I slide off the bed and stalk to the door, the stone floor cold and uneven beneath my feet. Instead of making a swipe for me, Tye moves to the other side of the room, which is odd in itself—as is the rest of this morning. Closing the latch, I turn to face both males. "What don't I know?"

Tye snorts. "A great many things. In this case, however, I imagine it isn't so much a lack of *knowledge* as a lack of appreciation that the fleabag on your bed is a predator. Shade's wolf mated with you last night."

I press my lips together. "Yes, I was there."

"Not just bedded, cub." Shade's voice is a low rumble.

"Mating is more, well, permanent."

Fire rakes through me as I wheel on the shifter. With me standing and him sitting on the bed, I can for once look him in the eye. "And did you not think I might want a say in the matter?"

"Shade didn't get a choice—why should you?" Tye says in such a reasonable tone that my fingers curl into fists. Tye's eyes flick to my clenched hands and he holds up his own, palms facing toward me. "I said Shade's *wolf* mated. It's an instinct, and it asks no one's opinion. It places no obligation on you."

I stalk over to the dresser. Clothes. I want clothes. And coffee. And a much better explanation than this charade. "If that were true, Tye, Shade wouldn't be in trouble, now would he?" I grab a set of undergarments and put them on beneath the cover of my bedsheet, ignoring the males' amused stares.

"I knew how close the mating bond was." Shade rises to his feet and rubs his face, his smoothly muscled body sending a familiar—and currently unwanted—need through my core. He slips into his black pants, still damp from last night. "I should have made it a point to stay away from you. At least until we could work out a plan."

"A plan for what?" I demand, tying the sash around my burgundy uniform tunic and bracing my hands on my hips.

"A plan for this." With no warning, Tye rushes forward and tackles me smoothly to the floor. His hands cup the back of my head, cushioning my fall, but there isn't time for more than that before a wolf's deadly growl pierces the room.

I gasp as Tye is knocked off me with enough force to make the redhead wince at the impact. Sitting up, I find Shade's wolf pinning Tye to the floor, white, salivating fangs snapping at the male's jugular.

"Stop!" I scream, my heart pounding. This is not a friendly fight, but a true, fevered assault.

Tye jerks and Shade's teeth miss his neck, piercing his shoulder instead. Blood soaks through Tye's tunic at once, dripping to the stone floor.

Fists pound against my latched door, and I sprint to open it, my breath catching as River and Coal burst inside.

River strides to the fighting pair, gray eyes thunderous, command oozing off him like a thick fog. "Leralynn, get out," he orders without looking at me.

I open my mouth to object, but Coal herds me out into the corridor, shutting the door behind us. Through the thick walls, I hear River command Shade to shift, the order so filled with power that even I shudder from the words' impact.

Something crashes.

"Move away." Coal pushes me toward the common room. Unlike me, tousled and still barefoot, the male is already crisply dressed and painfully handsome in his full uniform and black boots, his hair pulled back into a tight bun. He is also his usual, talkative self. "Your scent is little helping."

"My scent should be my own bloody business," I mutter. Sitting down on the leather sofa, I flinch at the crashes and grunts echoing from my bedchamber.

A few moments later, Shade—once more in his fae form

—storms out of my room and exits the suite altogether, slamming the door in his wake. River and Tye walk out next, Tye bare to the waist and pressing a towel against his shoulder as he settles on the couch beside me.

I reach toward him tentatively, relief flooding my body when he permits me to brush my fingers along his skin. "Was that because of me?" I whisper.

"That was Shade's wolf protecting his mate," River says curtly. His face is hard, making me sink further into the couch.

Tye places his good arm on my knee and shifts slightly to break the line of sight between me and River. "I goaded Shade on purpose, River. It was the easiest way to show Lilac Girl what a wolf's mating means." He offers me a smile. "It may seem like I think with nothing but my cock, but occasionally a thought does visit my head."

"Today was not one of those occasions," River snaps, pinching the bridge of his nose. His eyes survey the room, coming to rest on me in a long, stony stare. "Tye, wait until Shade cools off and then have him see to your shoulder. Leralynn, if you can manage without breakfast, I'd like us to claim the practice arena while the other trainees are still getting up and about. The senior quints have the authority to make us yield it, but I doubt anyone but Malikai will force the issue."

"What exactly are we going to the practice arena for?" I ask, already getting up to retrieve my boots.

"To train your magic, of course," says River.

I trip over my own feet.

14

RIVER

*T*he sun had just risen over the eastern Citadel wall, casting thin golden light across the empty square. A light breeze filled River's nose with Leralynn's lilac scent, making their walk from the trainee dormitories to the practice arena an exercise in self-control. She was in uniform, the fitted black trousers clinging to her hips in a sensual way that the tailor had never intended, her wine-red tunic slightly too large and showing the tops of her full breasts through the open V-necked collar. She'd braided her hair on one side, the neatly twisted strands like gleaming fire in the sun.

Just looking at the girl made River hard—which was not conducive to the day's plans. River tried to take shallow breaths, but it little helped. Leralynn's scent washed over him again and again. Potent, pulsing—and drenched with Shade.

Jealousy was not an emotion a good quint commander indulged in. River knew that. Agreed with it. Which did nothing to stop his heart from clenching rebelliously at the thought of Shade bringing Leralynn pleasure last night.

River hadn't brought a female pleasure in three hundred years; he wasn't even sure he knew how anymore.

"How long until Klarissa puts an end to this freedom?" Coal asked, surveying the Citadel's manicured grounds as if walking through a battlefield. It was early enough in the morning that most of the trainees and guests were still finding their way to breakfast, and only the occasional quint strode along the walkways. With each quint unique in both its needs and timing, the council issued specific training instructions for each group instead of hosting a one-size-fits-all curriculum. "I half expected to wake to a demand that we attend a lecture on Citadel power and law."

"I do not know." River clasped his hands behind his back, his face a careful mask of mild interest despite the blood in his veins screaming for Lera. In truth, River was surprised he could do it—walk beside her, talk, breathe. Perhaps it was something he could thank his bastard of a father for, training his body to control itself no matter its needs. To have a shred more self-possession than that damn wolf shifter.

Shade. As if the five of them didn't have enough problems in the Citadel without a half-feral and possessive wolf threatening to take over a trained warrior's common sense. A small growl escaped River's throat, making Leralynn flinch. Bloody wonderful. He made himself swallow a second growl that was already rising in his chest.

River would deal with Shade later, when River could be certain that it was his brain and not his cock that was restoring discipline.

A hand clamped onto River's wrist a second before the back of his head connected with a nearby tree trunk. An iron fist blocked River's return blow.

"If you can't train the mortal today," Coal said mildly, even as the dull thud of impact still echoed through River's body, "this would be a good time to say so."

River raised his chin, his voice calm despite his pounding pulse. "Is there a specific reason for this new concern, or have you simply gone too long without attacking something?"

Coal snorted, releasing River. "You just made the earth tremble and didn't even notice."

River's gaze jerked to the courtyard to find the few passing fae staring at him. Leralynn watched him with wide eyes, the fear there making his heart clench. An academic in long robes picked up books that River's jolt of power had knocked from her arms. Bloody cursed stars. So much for that self-control.

Coal raised a brow, his blue eyes twinkling.

Stepping away from the tree, River picked up his pace toward the practice arena, his face hot. "Let's move, Leralynn. The sun isn't waiting on anyone today," he called over his shoulder, leaving Coal to stand outside the arena and do what Coal did best: make anyone who wished to approach decide to do something less suicidal instead.

Leralynn made the climb up the stone steps and down the ladder rungs with little change to her breathing, something she never could have done before Coal's work with her. An odd pair if there ever was one. River had smelled blood on the girl more than once after one of Coal's "light combat" sessions, and yet Leralynn trusted the warrior. Certainly, she considered Coal more of a friend than she did River.

Leralynn considered everyone more of a friend than River.

His chest tightened. For Leralynn, the next few hours would be an exciting exploration of newly discovered power. For River, they'd be the first time he truly shared something with the girl, and his palms were as moist as a silly lad's. His breath quickened as he watched her turn about the sand, her eyes brushing the arena's circular wall, which rose fifteen feet into the air.

"So this is what standing at the bottom of a well feels like," Leralynn murmured.

"Remember that the walls are warded to ensure that whatever happens in here doesn't destroy the rest of the Citadel in the process."

"Convenient." Leralynn's chocolate eyes touched River's, sending a jolt of heat through him without even trying. "Can you set such wards anywhere?"

"Me? No." River squinted at the stone, inlaid with intricate runes. "Like many of the Citadel's wards— including the runes on your neck—these are much older and more powerful than we can create today. But if you are asking about wards in general, it is a studied art. Craftsmanship. Autumn is quite skilled, but I've never had the knack or the training for it." River trailed off, his gaze on Leralynn as a new worry bubbled inside his chest. She was small and perfect. And fragile and precious. Whereas the training . . . After the initial excitement wore off, it would be no less grueling than Coal's adventures with a blade.

There wasn't a choice on that score, not anymore, not with the damn runes tattooed right over her pulsing artery. The Citadel's magic had no back door, no escape route from the training grounds, bar the trials. Leralynn had to learn or die. And River would never let the latter happen, no matter how much she might come to hate him in the process.

They hadn't even started and he was already fretting. Bloody brilliant. River spread his shoulders, opening his mouth to issue his initial instructions—

"About Shade," Lera said.

River's mouth snapped shut.

"I realize you are angry. Can we—"

"We are not here to discuss Shade." River's hard words echoed from the circular walls.

Leralynn flinched—but didn't back down one bloody millimeter. "Right, let's pretend nothing happened. Good thinking."

"We are here to harness your magic so that you can stay alive, not discuss your bedmate choices," River snapped with more force than he'd intended. He stepped away toward the other side of the arena. It was bad enough that he had to smell Shade's scent all over her and deal with a feral wolf this afternoon. He didn't need the girl dragging Shade into their private training session too.

"Yes, about that magic . . ." Leralynn wrapped her arms

around herself, her tunic's open neckline sliding sideways to reveal the top of a delicate shoulder and supple skin. "We've a small problem there. Namely that I no longer have it."

"What?" River blinked. "Of course you have magic. I saw you use it. It no more appears and disappears than an arm does."

"Disappearing arms or not, I still don't feel it, River. Not like I did in the arena yesterday. I promise you, I've looked. There is nothing there."

"Look again."

Leralynn closed her eyes, the small movements beneath her lids suggesting that she was indeed looking. As if her magic was a toy someone had hidden from her in the darkness.

River waited. Seconds. Minutes. More than enough time for even a child to locate her own power—provided said child was paying attention. "I want you to focus on the well of power inside you," River said finally. "Let it nip you. Embrace its presence. Then tap it gently."

Leralynn opened her eyes, quirking one brow.

Making a quick motion with his hand, River parted the arena's sand to draw a line down the middle. "Your magic has an earth-based affinity, same as mine," River continued, his voice level. Even as he spoke, he quietly spiraled down into his own well of magic and readied himself to parry the inevitable disaster. Novices were prone to explosions, no matter how many times one told them to go easy. "Your task is to push a few grains of sand across the line. Precision, not strength." River readied his shield and braced himself. "Start now."

Leralynn closed her eyes again.

Silence rang through the arena.

"I said start," River pressed.

The girl's eyes finally popped open, brimming with frustration. "There is nothing to tap, no matter how much you wish it were otherwise."

River's jaw tightened. "This isn't about what I wish. This is about your body. Twenty-five pushups, then try again."

Leralynn let out a puff of air but lowered obediently to the sand. Her gorgeous body, its curves plain despite the oversized tunic, rose and fell to River's count. A shudder ran through him when she finished, sitting back on her knees in a way that gave him too good a view of the tops of her breasts. *Stars.* He forced his eyes away. If he wanted that body of hers to survive the trials, he needed to concentrate. He needed for them both to concentrate. "Get up," he said, jerking his chin toward her. "Feet shoulder-width apart, breathing steady, picture the magic inside you rumbling in its well. Tap the well, Leralynn. Grab hold of one strand."

Leralynn's furrowed brow provided little encouragement. The fact that nothing happened provided even less.

"Twenty-five pushups," River said, when Leralynn's eyes opened again with nothing but wasted time to show for the effort.

Another quarter hour of trying. Another set of pushups. Another cycle of growing frustration.

"I don't have magic," Leralynn growled finally, refusing —actually refusing—to follow his latest order.

"We are not debating reality."

The girl frowned. "You not wishing to debate the existence of my magic doesn't actually change the fact that it's not there."

River's jaw tightened. She wasn't trying, not truly. Wherever Leralynn's mind was just now, it clearly wasn't in the arena with him.

Most likely, it was still in Shade's bed.

Before he could tell her as much, Leralynn stalked toward him, her boots impertinently smudging the line in the sand that River had drawn. Tipping her head back, she glared at him, the heat from her body saturating the air between them. "I don't *have* magic, River," she said, her full lips enunciating each word as if it were *him* who was having trouble understanding reality. Stars. If defiance had a scent, River was certain it would reek of lilac. Leralynn tapped his chest, sending a jolt of heat through him. "Whatever you think you saw in the arena, it wasn't me following in your bloody magical footsteps. So you might as well demand that I wag my tail or wiggle my horns for all the good it will do."

River's heart pounded against his ribs, fire simmering in his veins and rising to his face. He longed to grab the girl and shake her. Or kiss her. Or both. His breath quickened. "In the past week, you've tricked the quint into a full connection, singlehandedly accepted the Elders Council's demands, and are now arguing with me over known facts because you find them inconvenient," he growled instead, returning the reckless sprite's glare with enough ire to make most fae warriors blanche. "You're stubborn, you know that? A damn stubborn mortal."

Not that it had any effect on her, stars take him.

Grabbing the hand Lera was jabbing him with, River leaned down until his face was inches from the girl's. Their breath mixed, her stray pieces of hair tickling River's neck, setting every nerve in his body alight. "You've a brash streak wide enough to make Tye pale in comparison, and so little sense of self-preservation, it's a bloody miracle you've survived as long as you have. And just now, I'm fed up with it." His words came hard and fast, a staccato of cold command. "Move. The. Sand. That's an order."

Leralynn narrowed her eyes, twisting her wrist free of River's grasp. Her heart was beating hard enough to make the skin beneath her runes pulse, the coiled storm in her glare matching River's own. "You want the sand moved?" Leralynn's soft voice sent a warning shiver down River's spine. Before he could answer, she stepped back and kicked the ground, her boot sending a fountain of sand all the way to River's chest. "It's moved. Magic."

The tether River had on his temper snapped.

15

LERA

$\mathcal{L}$ ightning flashes through River's gray eyes, his large body somehow bigger, more deadly than it was moments ago. His muscles coil against his deep-red shirt, the outline of lean power filling the arena. Pulsing through me.

For a heartbeat, I think I feel the magic he demanded, but then my eyes widen to reality as a whirlwind of sand rises from the arena floor at River's silent command. The grains spin, faster and faster, each rotation building on itself as the male steps away, his chest heaving.

The sand rises, reaching my calves, my shins, my waist. I bring up my hands, warding off the grains now pelting my skin, and glare at River from the heart of the whirlwind. "Stop it," I shout at him.

"You stop it," River barks back at me, his shoulders rising and falling with harsh breaths. His face, with its angled cheekbones and strong jaw, is focused on me and nothing else. Centuries of dominance back each word he throws into my face. "This isn't a dance, Leralynn. You have three runes on your neck now, and they will dissolve only through trials or death. Don't like sand pelting you? Shove it back. Throw up a shield. Send out a raw bloody blast of magic to the sky itself. Do *something*."

I open my mouth to shout right back at him, only to have the sand coat my tongue at once. My pulse races, mixing with my rapid breathing.

Bastard. *Bastard.* A royal princely ass who is so certain of himself, he can't be bothered to consider that I may not fit into his rules. His world. Because I don't fit. There is no magic inside me, no matter how impossible River claims that to be. The well of magic I felt in the trial arena isn't empty—it's gone altogether, leaving not even a shadow of what I once controlled.

"Do you know how little effort this is taking on my part?" River shouts while I struggle for each breath, the sand scratching my eyes. "I could do this all day. All night. Keep the sand pressing just enough to trap you here. No one can engage your magic for you, any more than they could take a shit on your behalf. So I highly recommend that you pull your head from Shade's bed, or wherever it's been for the past hour, and start fighting for yourself."

Shade's bed. I bare my teeth, heedless of the resulting sand coating my tongue. Blood rushes to my face, the skin on the back of my neck stinging from the onslaught. So that's what this is. Retribution. River shoving his bloody weight around because he's unhappy with Shade and me.

Because he wants his damn orders followed, for the whole bloody world to do as he ordains.

I'm done playing this game.

Turning my head away from River, I find the ladder rungs worked into the stone a few feet away. The male can throw his magical tantrum all he wants—I don't need to be around to witness it.

Keeping my face to the wall, I slide against the rock toward the footholds, each step a fight against wind and sand. My eyes water, the bits of sand in them irritating the sensitive tissue. A small whimper escapes my lips, but my hand closes over the first ladder rung in resounding victory.

Sand covers the metal rung at once, making me slip.

I fall to my hands and knees. My mind roars. Reaching inside myself, I claw for anything to block the assault. But there is nothing. No well of magic. No preternatural power. Only a little bit of pride that erodes more with each blast of sand in my face.

"I can't!" I shout, my voice raspy. *I can't,* the words echo inside me. I can't tap into magic, can't be what River wants, can't be enough of a quint warrior to escape the Citadel.

River crouches beside me, just outside the sandstorm. "Yes, you can," he says. So confident and certain that I want to punch him. "And when you truly want this to stop, you will."

RIVER

*R*iver let Leralynn climb out of the practice arena ahead of him, so she wouldn't see him smash his fist against the stone wall. A disaster. There was no more accurate way to describe the morning, the vast rift that had formed between him and the girl. River's head swam, and in the momentary privacy of the arena, he let his forehead press against the cool stone.

The last time River recalled failing so utterly was when he went to tell Daz about his newly forged quint bond, to beg the female he'd been in love with for years to stay with him. Daz had said no, and there was nothing in Lunos or the stars that River could do for it. And now, three centuries later, he was here again. About to lose the most precious thing in his life. A cold spike of fear stabbed his spine.

Maybe he *was* jealous. Shade was Leralynn's first true mate, and Tye was the one she trusted and played with.

Even Coal had a tether with the female, something deep and primal that only the two of them shared—for good and for ill. And River . . . River had wanted to be her first too. The first to guide her through the magic simmering in her veins, to watch her face light up when she discovered the new ways her magic let her speak with the world.

"River," Coal called over the wall.

With a final deep breath, River straightened himself, summoning the calm mask that his father's upbringing had taught him to wear. By the time he'd scaled the wall and come down on the other side, he was as certain that no one could read his thoughts as he was of the hate in Leralynn's eyes—red and irritated from the sand.

River glanced at Coal, whose face revealed nothing, and felt another stab of pain. Coal could do it. He could put Leralynn through violence and hell and leave her better, stronger, more trusting. River, it seemed, could only break and destroy. When she went into the arena next, would she even remember her own strength? Or only his antics?

"I'm going ahead," River said, skirting around Leralynn and Coal to beat the two to the suite. Now was about undoing the damage he'd just done—and the last thing Leralynn needed was more time in River's company.

"Shade!" River called as he banged open the door, relief flooding his senses when the wolf appeared. With his tail down and nose close to the ground, Shade looked very much like how River felt. River sighed. "Could you shift, please? I've no intention of discussing the mating just now."

The wolf hopped up on the couch, laid his fuzzy head on his paws, and blinked yellow eyes at River.

"Please?" River said through clenched teeth. "Leralynn is a few steps behind me. It . . . it was a rough training day."

That got Shade's attention. A growl escaped from deep within the wolf's chest as he hopped down to the floor and circled.

Good enough. "Take care of her when she comes," River said, heading to his own room. "I'll keep out of your way for as long as necessary."

A flash of light blinded River in the next moment. "Wait," Shade said, now in fae form. He rolled his shoulders, the muscles coiled so hard that a fine tremor raced over his skin. "Is her life in danger?"

"If you mean at this moment, then no—she is more sore than injured. If you mean later, in the arena, when she needs to use the magic I can't pull out of her, then yes." River made himself say each word. "She could use a friend just now, though."

"She has a friend," Shade said, blocking River's path. "I'm looking at him."

River's nostrils flared. "Did you not hear me? Leralynn is hurt, and I'm the one who bloody hurt her."

"Then you should be the one to bloody fix it." Shade's words were ragged, each a struggle against his instincts.

"I don't know how to fix it," River hissed.

Shade flinched as the door opened behind River to admit the girl and Coal. River didn't need to turn to know how red the girl's eyes were, how she leaned on Coal when she walked. Shade's breathing grew harsh, his heart racing so fast that River could hear it. "You are hers as much as I am," the wolf shifter murmured nonetheless, as Leralynn headed right for her bedchamber. "And you can fix your own messes."

A flash of panic seized River's chest. The bloody male was serious. He was going to leave. "Shade—"

"I'm meeting Tye for lunch early," Shade said, stepping away. "I don't imagine we'll see you at the dining hall." Before River could protest, a flash of light had Shade shifting into his wolf and loping out the door as quickly as his powerful legs could carry him.

Turning slowly, River faced the last being left in the common room and debated whether enlisting Coal's help might still be possible.

Coal cocked a brow.

Right. River might as well find a sclice and ask the Mors rodent for advice. "Excuse me," he said, and squaring his shoulders, he headed to Leralynn's bedchamber.

Only to stop outside her closed door, his limbs suddenly numb.

Stars. River had gone into battle without his heart racing as quickly as it did now. His hands were clammy against the doorframe. His knuckles rose to knock, then fell to the door handle instead. There seemed little point in requesting permission—River already knew he wasn't welcome. Drawing his last fortifying breath, he opened the door and stepped into the room.

Leralynn stood with her back to him, the sunlight slanting through the window silhouetting her curves. Her boots and pants lay in a sandy pile on the floor, the long tunic of her uniform reaching just below the mounds of her backside. He realized he'd never seen her pale, smoothly muscled legs before, and his mouth went dry. Her arms, already braced to pull off the garment froze in mid-motion.

"If you are looking for more sand to throw at me, it's on the floor," Leralynn said, pulling her shirt off and reaching for the washbasin beside her. Red, sand-scraped patches covered her back and arms, now bare but for thin undershorts and a chest band. A long, thin cut wound along the groove of her spine and circled like a tail along her lower back.

River's chest squeezed painfully. He'd done this to her.

Striding up behind her, River dipped a small towel into the washbasin. "I'm not apologizing," he said, dabbing the moist cloth carefully against the first of the scrapes. Leralynn flinched and River's left hand braced her abdomen reflexively, his fingers spreading wide over her smooth stomach. Her skin warmed under his hand, the muscles clenching as he dabbed the cuts, no matter how gentle he tried to be. Stars, she was small. Especially now, standing disrobed with her back to him, the top of her auburn head barely brushing his collarbone. River's palm alone covered most of the girl's torso.

"Thank you for clearing that up," said Leralynn. "For efficiency's sake, I suggest we skip the so-called instruction tomorrow and move directly to dragging me along the ground."

"If I thought it would help, I would do so in a heartbeat." He pressed the wet cloth against a raw patch of skin on her shoulder blade, biting the inside of his lip when she flinched. The fingers of his bracing hand traced tiny circles on her abdomen, a feeble attempt to distract the girl's mind from the sting. Breathing in slowly, River savored her lilac scent, now mixed with sweat, soreness, and musky stubbornness. "There are very few things I wouldn't do if I thought they'd help you walk out of the Citadel alive."

"As noble as that sounds, the gap between what you think would help and what would *actually* help is wide enough for a school of piranhas to slither through." Leralynn finally turned her head far enough to meet River's gaze. Her eyes still watered from the sand, the lids red and puffy beneath impossibly long lashes. "Why are you here, exactly?"

"Because Shade told me to clean up my own mess." River snapped his mouth shut, his face heating. He hadn't meant to say that. Half a millennium of training and fighting, and the crown prince of Slait Court could come up with nothing better to say.

"Your mess can clean up herself." Raising her chin, Leralynn moved the washbasin closer, trying and failing to hide a wince in the process. "I grew up in a stable, not a palace. I'm used to it."

River's chest clenched, his body no longer willing to acknowledge reason as Leralynn slipped from his fingers. He stepped toward her, the single pace of distance between them feeling like an abyss to be leapt blindly in hopes of finding the other side. Grasping Leralynn's hips, River lifted her from the floor and pulled her into his body. "Having grown up at a palace," River said over the pounding of his heart as he perched himself on the lip of the girl's bed, her small weight settled sideways on his lap, "I'm much more dainty about such things."

17

LERA

*M*y breath halts as River pulls my aching body against his chest, his muscled thighs warm and hard beneath my backside. His tunic scrapes my bare skin, the heat of his body wrapping itself around me with throbbing insistence. I can't move. The small reserve of bravado that fueled me to walk back to the suite and remove my sand-filled clothes emptied the moment River's calloused hand splayed across my abdomen.

I close my eyes, taking a deep, shuddering breath filled with River's clean, woodsy scent. I've never been here before, on River's lap. In his arms. It feels like settling onto a grand, intoxicating boulder. My heart pounds.

It isn't fair, how easily River carries power. He seems unaware of how large, how dominating, how bloody impenetrable he is. Born to rule, trained to command, chosen to lead elite warriors who can probably stare down armies. I couldn't so much as stare down Zake a couple weeks ago, and here I am, trying to stand toe to toe with the male who made the Elders Council uneasy. Not am—was. It's gone now, whatever strength I conjured in the arena, melted beneath the touch of a male who any smart human should fear.

"I was harsh with you," River whispers into my hair. More a confession than an apology.

If I could move, I'd elbow his square jaw and knee his groin and holler every vile insult I could think of into his pointy immortal ears. Instead, my cheek presses into the groove below his shoulder, nestling beside the large pectoral that pulses with his own rapid heartbeat. His skin is warm and velvety soft, so in opposition to the hard muscle—the hard male—underneath. Tears spill down my cheeks, soaking River's shirt.

"I'm not crying," I clarify.

"It's just the sand irritating your eyes," River agrees, his left arm holding me against him while his right hand rubs a small circle on the back of my neck.

After a few minutes of soothing silence, I reluctantly pull away enough to peek at River's face, bracing myself for either the pity or resigned disappointment that I know I'll find. A warrior prince looking down at a sobbing little mortal girl.

Except River isn't looking at me at all. No, River's strong face is tipped up to the ceiling, his jaw clenched tightly. The light from the window reflects in his gray eyes and shimmers in droplets of silver that line the male's lower lids. Threatening to spill onto his chiseled cheekbones.

My thoughts scatter, suddenly as irrelevant as tufts of dandelion. "River?" I press my palm against his face, feeling his warm, rough skin. "River, what's wrong?"

The male lowers his head, his lips pressed into a grim line.

I run my thumb over River's cheek, over the muscles in his jaw, urging them to relax. "What are you thinking about?"

The apple of his neck bobs for a moment, and I'm certain he won't answer. But he does. "I'm thinking that it's been three hundred years since I've held someone like this," he whispers, his eyes not meeting mine. "And that if you wanted to destroy me, all you'd have to do is walk out the door. And that, after this morning, you just might."

My chest tightens. Pulling my legs up beneath me, I rise onto my knees, straddling River's lap, and bring my face in line with his. Up close, his short brown hair looks tousled, with fine grains of sand hanging on disobediently curving strands. I brush the sand away, letting my fingers linger on River's tense brow. "I'm half-naked." I reach for a small smile. "It is highly unlikely that I'll be walking out of this room just now."

River's gaze finally touches mine, his eyes so full of need and fear that I don't recognize the hard quint commander behind them. Raising his hands, he pushes my hair away from my face and down my back, detangling it gently with his fingers. The slight tugging is divine against my scalp. Then his calloused palms trace the length of my neck, my shoulders, my aching arms.

My skin tingles, each touch of River's fingers leaving a trail of warmth.

"We aren't going back into the practice arena tomorrow," River whispers. "Or ever. Not like that."

I swallow. "Why?"

River's voice is raw. "Because I won't risk you hating me."

I grip his eyes and lean in, my nose almost touching his. "Coward."

A startled growl vibrates through his chest.

"I'm not walking away from you, River," I say, keeping my face where it is, my heart pounding. "And you sure as hell aren't walking away from me."

Before he can reply, I press my lips against his, feeling his caught breath all the way through me. Cupping River's rough cheeks, I deepen the kiss, claiming his mouth—claiming him—with an intensity that has him gasping.

River's hands still, his whole body going rigid before suddenly waking with a surge. He pulls away, his eyes wide as his broad chest heaves. "Leralynn," he whispers, his free hand tangling in my hair as he tips my head back and captures my lips with his own.

My scalp tingles, River's command of my mouth and body taking on his usual warrior's confidence. His power. The longing of three hundred years in each strong, skilled stroke of his tongue. One hand cups the back of my head, the other tracing a hot, rough path up my bare side, covering my wrapped breast, tracing my collarbone, then hooking around my waist and pulling me closer.

I feel his hardness rise beneath me and suppress a gasp.

His woodsy scent, his taste—masculine and strong—fill my senses. I melt into the warrior, my aching body surrendering to his control as prickles of what can only be River's magic caress my skin.

As if in response to that yield, River palms my hips with both hands, pulling me closer still, possessing me, as our hearts thunder together. Hard. Harder still. Until only the need to draw breath pulls us apart.

MY MOUTH IS as sore as the rest of me when River, Coal, and I walk toward the mess hall an hour later. With my first-trial uniform still filled with sand, I'm wearing my normal training outfit—black leather pants, tall boots, and another one of Autumn's perfectly fitting jewel-toned tunics, this one a rich plum. Cutting my eyes to River, I find his dark hair brushed back into perfect place, his eyes once more an opaque gray.

If a kiss leaves Tye grinning roguishly and Shade quietly pleased, River seems like a male who's just stepped away from mortal combat, the energy rolling off him intense enough that even Coal gives us a wide berth.

My own body fares little better, my emotions and needs and logical thoughts waging a silent war of their own. Kissing River felt like welcoming an avalanche, the aftershocks of which still make my chest tremble.

Just as we approach the door, Tye and Shade are making their way out. I set an intercept course, but Coal lays a firm hand on my elbow, his eyes unyielding. "Give

Shade the rest of the day, mortal," he says quietly, steering me away. "You aren't injured, but you are sore and he smells that well enough. He smells River on you too. Adjusting to his instincts is more difficult than you can imagine."

I sigh but wait until Tye and Shade are out of sight before following River and Coal toward the meat table.

"First Trial," Malikai's too-loud voice rings through the hall, his pale eyes on River as he stretches his long legs into the walkway, ankles crossed. His black hair is pulled back in a low bun, accentuating his sharp widow's peak. "I need my dirty dishes carried off. Trot to it."

The hall goes silent, except for an errant spoon that rings once against a saucer. My muscles tighten, the tension in the room suddenly thick enough to choke a bear.

Malikai wiggles his ankles expectantly.

With all eyes on him, River turns to the male, looking down at Malikai from his greater height. With River's broad shoulders and cut jaw, he seems to fill up the hall, the Citadel, the world. A prince, no matter what uniform he wears.

The apple of Malikai's neck bobs as he swallows, and he raises his chin.

Coal's hand, which I hadn't realized was gripping my wrist, tightens further, firm as a shackle.

"Of course," River says calmly. He bows and strides over to Malikai's table, picking up a heaping plate of discarded bones and filthy napkins.

Malikai holds up a hand, halting the prince in mid-motion. "On second thought," the third trial says, the corners of his mouth curling. "I would like the female to tend to me."

"You are welcome to like anything you want, sir," River says mildly. "It little means you will get it."

Malikai's grin dissolves. "I've issued an order, First Trial." The words are low, the threat in them sending a jolt of fear down my spine.

Plate still in hand, River straightens, his movements too slow and controlled to be safe. I'm not sure what happens to fae who disobey orders from their theoretical superiors, but having glanced at the whipping post outside, I'm not eager to find out. Even with my blood still simmering from the practice arena, the thought of anyone harming my males makes acid crawl up my throat.

"Did you hear me?" Malikai says.

River's eyes flash dangerously.

"I can take care of dishes as well as the prince of Slait can," I say. Pulling away from Coal, I stride across the silent dining hall in hopes of unraveling this disaster before tempers spill into fists. River's muscles are coiled as I take the dirty plate from his hand and carry it over to the counter, where I saw the others dropping their trays for the kitchen staff.

"Damn clumsy of me," Malikai sings behind my back. "I've spilled the wine. Fetch that rag beside you and mop it up, will you, human?"

Right. This game. Taking one of the kitchen towels from the counter, I return to Malikai's table as carefully as if I were walking through a field of booby traps, lest River and Coal lose their tentative grip on the violence brewing beneath their skin. The others in the hall have stopped even pretending to eat, and now watch the confrontation playing out with the morbid fascination of one watching a rider cling to a rearing horse—simultaneously dismayed and unable to turn away.

I make myself smile at Malikai. A jest, that's all this is. Bothersome, and perhaps malicious, but a jest nonetheless. Wiping up wine spilled on a table is, after all, hardly the height of humiliation. Laying the towel over the puddle, I watch the rich liquid soak into the white cloth, turning it pink.

Malikai's hand tips a second glass, this one closer to him.

A harsh intake of breath that I'm sure is Coal's echoes through the hall, but I just mop up the new mess without comment, humming a tune to myself as I do.

A third glass tips, this time making the wine run off the table and onto Malikai's lap, soaking his trousers. The male grins, spreading his thighs. "Keep cleaning, human."

My breath catches. Before I can utter a word, a hand clamps over my wrist and a familiar metallic musk fills my nose.

Coal takes the towel from my hand. "What did you need, exactly, Malikai?" Coal's voice is very, very soft, his blue eyes brimming with a violence that makes my mouth dry. "I'll be happy to assist you from here."

18

LERA

$\mathcal{M}$alikai freezes for a heartbeat, his gaze flicking from the wine-soaked towel, to his own soiled breeches, to the deadly warrior now standing before him with a single brow cocked in question.

Let it go, I beg the males, my pulse pounding in my ears. *Enough.*

Malikai grins, showing sharp canines. "Ah. Coal, isn't it? I've heard of you."

"I'm flattered."

"Sir." Malikai clicks his tongue. "I'm flattered, *sir.* That's the proper address. No matter, I've more pressing questions I've been meaning to ask you, specifically." He stretches slowly, interlacing his hands behind his head. Keeping Coal waiting. Stars. The rules of the Citadel's hierarchy must be ironclad indeed for Malikai to feel safe when most sentient beings would be hunkering down from the murder lurking in Coal's blue eyes. Malikai jerks his chin at Coal's hand. "Give the rag back to the girl. You are much too valuable for mopping up spills. I understand you've firsthand experience of Mors—experience that all at the Citadel would benefit from knowing. Tell me . . ." Malikai pauses to lick his canines. "Tell me, did your keepers fuck you while you were there, or were they not into that sort of thing with livestock?"

I'm swinging my fist at Malikai's face before I can think through the wisdom of it. The wisdom of attacking a fae quint leader in the middle of a hall filled with other immortals.

"Leralynn! No!" River bellows, lunging for me as the world slows to a mocking crawl.

Malikai marks my coming fist and, instead of blocking it, opens his face to the blow—all but aiming his eye to connect with my knuckles. His grin widens.

Coal, who is closest, shoves me so hard that I tumble over my own feet and slide across the polished floor. Standing where I was a moment ago, Coal now leans down to bring his face so close to Malikai's that the latter has the good sense to blanche. "I imagine you will discover the pleasures of Mors soon enough, Third Trial." His voice is sharpened steel. "I wouldn't wish to ruin the surprise."

My heart pounds in the silent hall. I climb to my knees and feet, breathing hard, while Coal steps away from Malikai, whose chest seems to expand in relief. Before I can take a step, however, an arm that belongs to none of my males grips my hips.

"I believe a third trial ordered you to clean his

breeches," an unfamiliar voice says, shoving me forward into Malikai's lap. My face slams into the wine-soaked fabric around his crotch.

"Oh, you are back." Malikai's hand clamps onto the back of my head, keeping me in place despite my struggle to rise. "See anything you like? Please have a feel if—"

The crash of an overturned table is the first sign that the world beyond Malikai's crotch still exists. Malikai's scream of pain is the second. I'm pulled away by River's familiar hands just in time to see Coal's fist strike Malikai's jaw a second time. The blow lands hard enough to elicit an audible crack of bone.

Malikai drops to all fours, one hand trying to stanch the flow of blood from his mouth.

Grabbing Malikai's now-empty chair, Coal breaks the wood easily over his knee, thrusting the two jagged legs against Malikai's throat like daggers. Coal's eyes are dark, the blue in them a deep, feral sapphire that is hungry for violence.

"Stand . . . down . . . First Trial," Malikai says, straining to speak through his broken jaw, the words pushed out desperately as blood pours from his mouth onto his tunic. "I order—"

Coal twists, sinking the back of his heel into Malikai's abdomen.

As if set loose by an open floodgate, the rest of Malikai's quint, including the male who shoved me into Malikai's lap, rush forward.

The chair legs in Coal's hands move so quickly, they're a blur of wood that sends the first of the attackers to the floor, a bloody gash crossing his chest from left hip to right shoulder. His gasp of pain cuts through the room.

River's hold on me tightens, my heart racing.

The second male stumbles over his fallen companion. Grabbing the back of the second's head, Coal spins the male in a wide arc, using the circular force's momentum.

The third male's eyes widen, his attempt to sidestep coming too late. Ice crackles in Coal's blue eyes as he slams the forehead of the spinning male into the new one's nose. Both males crash into a nearby table, sending bits of meat and porcelain into the air.

River's arms cover my head, shielding me from the debris.

The fourth male, the only one of Malikai's quint left standing, holds up his hands.

Coal tosses a chair leg from his left hand to his right and advances on the trembling male, blue eyes flashing with murder. Coal's arm cocks and—

The air thickens to the consistency of sour cream, just like it did when River surrendered in the arena.

My heart stutters. I can't move. Can barely breathe. Before me, Coal is stuck mid-motion, his eyes blazing. The other combatants, too, are held in their own odd and frozen poses.

"I see we have a small problem here," Elder Elidyr says with a sigh, his thick brown braid swaying as he looks around the once-pristine dining hall. Splatters of blood, food, plates, and trainees litter the floor. "May I trust all parties involved to act like civilized children once I release the hold?"

No one moves or speaks. None of us can.

Elidyr snaps his fingers.

The air loosens, River releasing me immediately to grab Coal, while a few others form a line between us and Malikai's quint. Not that anyone seems inclined to fight anymore. Or speak. The dining hall now holds its collective breath while the council elder shakes his head.

"Malikai," Elidyr says, waiting until the male has risen painfully to his feet. "I walked in to what appeared to be a single first trial pummeling your whole third-trial quint into a spineless pancake. Would you agree with that assessment?"

Malikai bows.

River's jaw tightens, a muscle ticking on the side of his face.

"Report to the infirmary, Malikai, and then wait in my office." Elidyr turns to River, the elder's eyes kind as he spreads his palms. "I'm sorry, River. I imagine you are aware of what happens next?"

"Yes, sir." River's answer sends a shiver down my spine. "Would next bell be acceptable?"

Elidyr nods, turning toward the door.

"Malikai." Coal's soft voice carries the promise of murder, stopping the injured male in his tracks. "It's fortunate that the trials need not be taken in order. I look forward to . . . facing you in the arena."

All the color drains out of Malikai's face.

19

TYE

"I'm fine, Shade," Tye said, trying and failing to pull his shoulder from the male's grasp. The bite was deeper than Tye had expected and the flesh was still weeping. "You already saw to it this morning."

"Take off your shirt or I'll tear it off." Shade pushed Tye down onto the couch's armrest. "It's a bite. You don't know where the wolf's mouth has been."

"*You* know where it's been," Tye said, throwing up his hands. "It was your bloody mouth."

Shade flashed his canines. "Which lends weight to my insistence that we keep a close eye on the wound."

Tye pulled his shirt off. "I hope you were more charming when you talked Lera out of her clothes."

Shade flinched, but it was much too late for that. Despite the whole morning apart, Leralynn's lilac scent drifted from the shifter in waves. For once, however, Tye little minded. He'd had enough females over the years and would have the lass when she wanted him for more than curiosity or instinct—if she ever did.

Females, in Tye's experience, saw through him all too easily. He was the kind of male they tumbled with for fun, not the kind they wished to share a life with. The lowest in the quint's hierarchy, Tye had nothing. No rank, no title, no property that he'd not stolen. He was a short-lived amusement in females' lives—the one Lera had gone to for instruction, not emotion. For the first time in his life, Tye little wanted to be *that* male. He wanted a bond. Love. Tye wanted to mate.

The very high probability of this never happening . . . *That* Tye did mind. Very much.

He also very much minded the jar of green medical goo Shade was reaching for. The stuff stung like a lash. "Touch me with that and I'll roll in Lera's underclothes and stay outside your door all night. See how well you sleep with that bonny bouquet filling your nose."

"I imagine I'll have to get used to it sooner rather than later. Though it was almost worth it just to see River's face when we left for lunch." Shade cracked open the jar and lathered the hell-in-liquid-form over the punctures, sending a healing pulse along with the salve. For such a deadly predator, he truly did hate watching others in pain. Most of the time. "I don't recall seeing him quite so afraid before."

"I counted all limbs present when we passed them," Tye said through clenched teeth. "But with some luck, we'll still catch some sparks between them this evening."

Shade tried for a smile and failed miserably. "What the bloody hell am I going to do?"

"What the bloody hell *did* you do?" asked a familiar feminine voice from the doorway as River's sister, Autumn, let herself into the suite. Dressed in sapphire silk trousers and a top that stopped at her ribcage, the female shimmered with an energy as brilliant as the emerald-and-diamond stud piercing her navel. Her hair, braided along her scalp in many silver-blond strands, sparkled with golden thread. Her sharp gray gaze narrowed on Tye's shoulder. "If those are teeth marks, I do hope it was Lera who left them."

Tye felt a grin taking over his face. "When Lera bites me, she won't be aiming for my shoulder, Sparkle," he said, rising to spin the petite female in the air.

A second female voice—this one still outside—dissolved into a coughing fit.

"You can bite me too, Kora, if you'd like," Tye called as he set Autumn back on the floor. "It seems to be the day for it."

"I wouldn't be biting your shoulder either," Kora called back in a way that made Tye close his legs. Walking inside, the female set down the pile of books that accompanied Autumn everywhere she went and backed away. Her gaze— which, in a just and righteous world, would be brushing Tye's shirtless torso—was instead working very hard to avoid Autumn's curves. "She came out of the Gloom *inside* the Citadel somehow," Kora said. "And asked for you when my patrol challenged her."

"Actually, I asked whether any quints were severed recently," Autumn said, dropping her cloak, bag, gloves, and a half-eaten sweet roll on various previously empty surfaces —bringing chaos to a tidy room with preternatural efficiency. "And once I was satisfied that you lot somehow scraped together enough wit to not let that girl from your sight, then I asked after you. Granted, I hadn't expected to find you back in trainee garb. Good stars. What the bloody hell happened?"

"Excuse me," Kora said with a polite bow, letting herself out.

"Well?" Autumn invited herself onto the couch, pulling her legs under her as she fixed her sharp eyes on Tye. "If you don't tell me exactly what's going on, kitty cat," she said sweetly, "I'm going to tell Lera that the marks still on your shoulder are a symptom of fae pox."

Tye grabbed his shirt, pulling it on quickly. "I sent you a message yesterday," he said through the fabric. He sat down opposite her on the low table. "Which I imagine will be arriving at the Slait palace imminently. But the short answer to your question is that everything that could possibly go wrong either already has or is simply waiting its turn."

"You've been at the Citadel for two and a half days," Autumn said. "How much trouble could you possibly have gotten yourselves into in two and a half bloody days?"

Tye held up a hand, ticking things off on his fingers as he spoke. "Klarissa made us into rune-bearing trainees on the ridiculous grounds that Lera's mortality makes us a brand-new quint. Shade mated with Lera and can think with nothing but his cock unless the female is out of the room. Lilac Girl developed magic with an earth-based affinity, which she can only access when it's convenient, to piss off River—"

"Lera hasn't developed magic," Autumn said calmly. "She is human. That's what I was catching up to tell you. That while Lera has no magic, it doesn't mean she can't use or at least bear magic. You may be able to connect the full quint."

Tye glanced at Shade. "You are right on the connection. We, well *she* . . . When we faced a school of piranhas . . . It's a long story. Why are you staring at my neck?"

Autumn wasn't just staring. She had risen up on her knees for such a careful examination that Tye was starting to feel like a potential dinner option. Extending her hand, Autumn traced one of the runes tattooed over his jugular. "I've seen that mark before," she said, pulling out one of the leather-bound volumes Kora had carried in. The same book she'd been studying when they were last at the Slait palace, if Tye recalled correctly. At her shooing motion, Tye obediently surrendered his space on the low table, stepping away while Autumn flipped through the earmarked pages. "Yes. Here. Except this is only a theoretical symbol. A story illustration." She slipped off the couch, heading right out for the door. "Tell the others I'm here and that I'll see them shortly. I need the library."

"Of course you do," Tye muttered at Autumn's receding back. "Who wouldn't want a library?"

The female threw a vulgar gesture over her shoulder before stepping out the door.

"Thank the stars she is here," Tye told Shade, sinking into the couch once the door closed behind Autumn's lithe form. There were few things in Lunos Tye could count on absolutely, but the fact that River's sister would take care of the heavy thinking topped the short list. More to the point, after witnessing the small female teaching Coal to read, Tye felt confident in saying there was nothing Autumn couldn't do.

Except decently cheat at cards. But no one was that perfect.

20

LERA

"What happens next?" I demand, following the silent males back toward our suite. My pulse pounds, the sound of my own rushing blood filling my ears. "What happens at the next bell?"

"Procedural matters," Coal says. "Nothing of consequence."

I step in front of Coal, blocking the male's path. Coal's eyes, now a flat, hard blue, slide around me to rest somewhere down the hall. I cross my arms. "Horseshit. It's something of enough consequence that Malikai expected it to provide him immunity."

"No, he didn't." River's voice is low, his jaw a hard line as he steers me around Coal. "He was simply willing to take a blow in order to trigger one of the penalties. Coal humiliated him when we arrived. Now Malikai will get to watch him be shackled to a whipping post. It was a planned provocation."

My mouth dries, a gut-churning dread filling my lungs. Phantom shackles clamp over my raw wrists, pain from another place, another world, washing over me. I gasp, shaking myself back to now.

"Whatever silliness you are imagining is incorrect," Coal says, lengthening his strides. "I'm an immortal—we heal faster than humans. I won't remember the lashes by tomorrow morning."

I grip River's thick wrist, holding him back. Shadows of screams only I can hear echo in my ears. "Coal is lying," I say as quickly and quietly as I can. "You need to stop this. Have the council do something else. Anything else. Please."

River sighs, gently tucking a strand of hair behind my ear. "I can't stop it, Leralynn. I can refuse to administer the penalty, but the council will simply find someone else to do it. But Coal is right—a couple dozen cuts, with Shade's magic helping, will heal quickly. This is more about the ceremony of it, the reminder of who is in charge. And who is not. A very sharp reminder."

I release his wrist, my gaze on Coal's back as the dread in my chest grows to a cold, gaping hole. River is wrong about what it will do to Coal. I know it. Except I can't explain why. Can't understand it myself.

"You shouldn't come to watch," River says gently. "I don't imagine Coal would appreciate more of an audience than will gather already. That's the true damage Malikai was going for—though if I know Coal, the show will be quite anticlimactic."

Right. Of course. Making a noncommittal noise, I start walking back to the suite.

Shade and Tye meet us at the door, Tye's attempt to tell us something drowned out by the wolf shifter's lunge for me.

"Cub," Shade rasps, his chest heaving as he cups my face with his wide palms. His yellow eyes gaze deep into mine, his thumbs tracing my cheeks with a desperation that makes my chest tighten. For a heartbeat, the world fades but for Shade's body heat, his scent of earth and rain. Shade braces his forehead against mine, the need inside him echoing through my blood. Shade draws a slow, desperate breath, like a man seeing water after days of drought. "Cub," he repeats as a gentle pulse of magic ripples through my flesh, making the scrapes along my skin tingle and pull until my ache dissolves and a relieved breath finally escapes Shade's lungs.

"I thought you were leaving that to me," River says dryly.

Shade pulls away, his shoulders tense. "I . . ."

"You couldn't help it." River squeezes the shifter's shoulder, eliciting a surprised brow tilt from Tye. "And we're about to have more work for you."

"What do you mean?" Shade brushes my hand one more time before reluctantly stepping away, his shoulders spreading as he transforms from gentle to deadly within a single heartbeat. "What happened?"

"A fight," Coal says, stepping out of his room. Wearing his signature black leather pants and sleeveless tunic, his blond hair in a tight bun, the warrior is a portrait of bored patience. "Why is the common room a mess and smelling of Slait?"

Tye picks up a half-eaten sweet roll and stuffs it into his mouth. "Sparkle is here. Well, not here—in the library. Because who would want to say hello to her brother when there are books to be read. But returning to other news, did I hear that right? Someone is going to be punished and it isn't me?"

"I'll be happy to bleed you tomorrow if you are envious," Coal tells him.

Tye opens his mouth, the tip of his tongue making a leisurely exploration of his canines. "As tempting as that is," he drawls, "I must admit that my own pleasures run a wee bit differently."

"Oh, good stars." Twisting on his heels, River stalks to his bedchamber.

I retreat to the couch, sinking into the soft cushions, the joy over Autumn's arrival unable to penetrate the flood of dread drowning my soul. Coal was a *slave* in Mors. Everything about this is wrong. Vile. Except no one but me seems to think much of it. Most notably Coal himself, who now leans against the wall with deadly grace, using a boot knife to clean his nails. The muscles in his arms bunch and slide with the small movements, and I long to go stand by him. Touch him, comfort him—but I know I'd just be comforting myself.

Coal wants my touch on him as little as he wants my thanks for pulling me off Malikai's lap.

My breath catches as Coal's blue eyes find mine. The male crooks a finger to call me over. When I oblige, he gazes down at me. "Your old master liked to use a belt on you, if I recall?"

I nod, a cold shiver running down my spine even as I lean closer, focusing my attention on whatever Coal wants to say. Needs to say.

Coal snorts softly. "Well, I'm not you, mortal. So stop projecting your personal little terrors onto me. It's embarrassing."

I snap away from him, the chill in my spine turning to ice. "Bastard." I twist away, my heart pounding as I stalk to the couch. *Bastard. Bastard. Bastard.*

The couch shifts as a wolf's soft paws land upon it, the animal circling before curling up against me, his warm, fuzzy head resting in my lap. I run a hand down his back and feel his rumble of pleasure.

A bell tolls in the distance and River returns to the common room. His hair is washed, and in place of a training tunic he wears a formal uniform, his blue jacket buttoned to the neck and a golden braid encircling one shoulder before looping across his broad chest.

"Pretty," Coal says, looking the prince up and down.

"It's the least I could do," River replies.

Coal snorts again, the two walking out the door as if heading to a dinner party.

In the silence that settles, Tye braces his arm on the back of a chair opposite me and tilts his head at Shade, who, I discover to my own surprise, I'm scratching between the ears. My hand stills. The wolf yips unhappily. The scratching resumes.

"Useless flea transport," Tye grumbles at Shade. "I take

it I have the pleasure of telling Autumn what happened?"
He pushes away, stopping a pace short of the door. "If
River and Coal return before we do," he says, turning to
look at me over his shoulder, "you may wish to let Shade
care for him alone. Coal isn't one to enjoy company when
he's hurt. When it's me—and note that I say *when*, not *if,*
because I think everyone knows I'll do something stupid
sooner or later—when it's me, please feel free to sit by my
side. You can brush my hair too; that always feels nice. And
feel free to say soothing things about how tight my muscles
are, how brave I am, how large my—"

Shade growls and Tye leaves at once.

Five minutes after that, I start screaming.

21

LERA

My wrists are shackled, the metal cutting into my raw skin promising of worse to come. My heart pounds at the sight of those iron bands, sweat beading on my forehead and draining down my face. There is no use pulling against the binds, but I do, ripping away skin. My breath comes so quick that I'm dizzy, unable to fill my lungs properly before the next breath. My hands shake. Tremble. My whole body shakes and trembles.

The click of boots against the cell's hard floor is muffled, as everything is in the Gloom. The qoru like it here.

"This is the bull?" one voice says to his companion. "Is it not a bit . . . rabid?"

"I was under the impression you preferred them this way."

A strip of blazing pain explores my left shoulder blade. Swallowing a scream, I twist to gaze at the male. He's naked, of course, his gray lizard-like skin stretched tight over bulging shoulders. He bounces on webbed hind legs, his milky pink eyes blinking hungrily, the round maw of piranha-like teeth opening in a perverted grin. The qoru takes a step toward me and I pull against the shackles until—

"Lera!" Arms shake me, Shade's yellow eyes level with mine as he crouches on the floor, to which I've somehow slid. "Look at me, cub. What's happening?"

"Coal," I manage to say, my mouth dry as I blink away a bad dream that's already fading from memory, my hands shaking with fear—the source of which my consciousness no longer recalls. Terror and pain wash over me in a phantom fog that has my breath catching in my chest. "I . . . don't think Coal is all right."

"He is all right," River says through the door, bringing both Shade and me to our feet. Behind the quint commander, Coal walks stiffly but without assistance, his black shirt looking merely wet instead of soaked in blood. For the first time, I think I understand his usual all-black clothing choice. If you can't see a warrior's blood, you can't see his weakness. "Malikai is disappointed at the lack of sound, but he'll get over it, I imagine."

Shooting me a worried look, Shade jerks his head toward his sleeping chamber. "I've the worktable set up. Come."

Left alone for a few moments, I take a deep breath. Then I follow the males, my heart still beating too quickly. By the time I enter, Coal is already lying on his stomach on the table. With no shirt to stanch the wounds, blood flows from his wide back onto the wood, filling the room with a coppery scent. A bowl of water beside Coal's shoulder is tinged the same crimson as the balled-up cloth floating inside.

River gets the hell out of my way as I step up beside Shade and rest a hand on Coal's shoulder, relieved to find the full extent of the damage hidden beneath a thick coat of Shade's shimmering magic. Coal's eyes are pale and open, staring emotionlessly through the far wall. Sweat beading at his temples is the only sign he's in any pain at all. His tattoo is hidden by the magic as well, the intricate lines that run down the length of his spine now surely in tatters.

"Leralynn—" River says tentatively.

I glare up at him, silencing the male in an instant. The world sways in rhythm with my pounding, simmering blood. Whatever the others think, whatever *Coal* himself thinks, he should never have been trapped against a whipping post. Not him. Not after Mors. My heartbeat echoes through my muscles, my skin, my soul, each new wave more powerful than the last. The hand I have on Coal's shoulder tightens, my energy flowing through—

Coal lets out a short, pain-filled curse.

"What did you do?" I demand of Shade.

"Not me, cub," Shade says quietly, his body shifting to bend around mine. His voice is soft, hypnotically calm—at odds with River's sharp intake of breath. Shade's hands settle atop my own. "Ease your magic. We want to mend the wounds from the inside, not sear the skin shut on the surface. We've time to go slow, not hurt him more than we must."

Shade's words ricochet inside me even as I feel him cajole the power that I can't deny is pulsing beneath my fingers.

"Don't be afraid," Shade says into my ear. Calm and

sure and confident. "I'll guide you. Feel along with me." Without moving either of our hands, I feel Shade's magic steer my own along paths I've never felt before, but which now feel as wide as carriage roads.

I lose track of time, the pulsing magic inside me ticking along with my heart and Shade's gentle commands. A power that is mine but not mine extends like a limb, probing damaged flesh, sometimes urging it to live and other times searing a tiny part closed to stanch a bleed or clear a bit too mangled to revive. Coal makes no sound, though I can tell the latter hurts him, and after guiding me through several closures, Shade takes those for himself.

The world tips and sways, strong hands gripping my elbows before I can fall. "That's enough for the first time," River says into my ear, pulling me out of the room. "Shade can finish up. Let us get some fresh air."

I follow along obediently, blinking at the breeze as my awareness returns. "Did I just . . ." I trip on the words.

"Use your magic?" River says. "Yes. And quite a great deal of it."

"You really should get out of the habit of talking about things you don't understand, River," Autumn says, coming up beside us and throwing her arms around me. "Lera didn't use *her* magic. She used Shade's."

WITH SHADE still working on Coal's back, Autumn, River, Tye, and I settle around the common room. Tye resourcefully procures a bottle of whisky, putting a tot in my hand before I'm fully aware of what's happening.

I wrap my hand around the drink, blinking at Autumn. *Autumn.* Here and real and—I squeal, launching myself at the small female, my arms going around her as Tye industriously rescues the whisky from my hand.

I can feel the female's grin, her braids tickling my neck. When I start to pull back, her hands tighten in one more embrace before letting me go. "Thank the stars," Autumn says, grinning back at me. "For a moment there, I wasn't sure you were going to let anyone near you."

I sigh. "It's been an . . . unusual day."

Autumn snorts and holds her empty glass out to Tye for a refill. "Don't jest with yourself, Lera. When it comes to these four, there is never a *usual* day. Speaking of which, do I want to know where exactly this whisky came from?"

Tye grins. "Your father has a fine taste for alcohol."

A smile I didn't think would ever return tentatively touches my face.

Catching my eye, Tye nods and extends my drink back to me.

Autumn rolls her eyes and pulls her bare feet under her, her loose blue trousers billowing around her legs. A circle of tiny gems glints in her exposed naval. "Now, then," Autumn says, sipping her drink. "Given that I don't believe the quint magic made a mistake in bonding the five of you, I started wondering why it chose you five, specifically. What's the connection? It was Coal's odd relationship with magic that got me thinking."

"What is odd about Coal?" I ask.

Autumn grins and Tye sucks in a long-suffering breath. "Don't ask questions, Lilac Girl. She'll talk your ear off and bore me to death."

"Magic is somewhat like blood," Autumn starts, her gray eyes sparkling. "It keeps us fae immortal, quickly healing and, in the case of shifters, able to change form. After basic bodily needs are met, we can use the excess magic externally for things like fire and earth manipulation, healing, and throwing up shields. Everyone except Coal, that is. His magic never leaves his body. It stays inside him, making him even stronger and faster than typical fae."

"I imagine it's how he survived Mors as long as he did," River says. "The qoru feed on their slaves' energy, but because Coal's is turned inward, they couldn't tap it."

My whole body tenses. Tye pulls me from my seat beside Autumn to press me against his chest, his pine-and-citrus scent brushing over me.

"Then there is the power of opposites," Autumn continues. "The notion that combining different things creates a stronger whole than combining similar things. You can do more with a bow and arrow than you can with two bows or two arrows alone."

"What does this have to do with me?" I ask.

"If Coal's magic is all inside," Autumn says, "I started wondering if Lera might be his opposite—able to manipulate only outside magic. It would make sense, since humans have no internal magic."

"She used my magic in the first trial, then," River says slowly. "And just now, she used Shade's to heal Coal's back."

A shiver runs through me. "I'm a parasite?"

"No, a symbiot," says Autumn. "The bow to the males' arrows. That's what I've been chasing after you to explain. But when I arrived and saw the runes on Tye's neck, I realized it was even more powerful than that." Leaning forward, Autumn flips through her book to a drawing of a five-corded rope that circles in on itself. "Quint magic is based on a power of five. A combination of five strands that creates a stronger whole than each one could alone."

"But our mark has four cords, not five." I swallow. "One is missing."

"Not missing, Lera." Autumn grins. "Simply opposite. A complement instead of a duplicate. The males' power is represented by the four cords, yours by the knots that the cords make. It isn't a new concept, just one that Lunos hasn't seen before."

"And here I thought I knew what 'new' means," Tye mutters.

Autumn taps her book. "I mean that it's been theorized. Predicted. Speculated about enough to be given a name. Didn't the man holding you, Lera, think the fae were coming for him?"

I frown, nodding slowly. "Zake believed he was destined for immortality. I don't think he thought it through more than that when he built his estate at Mystwood's edge."

The female grins. "I agree. But he likely was basing his delusions on old tales, legends that once came out of Lunos but morphed and changed since. Your rune has four cords because the fifth power, you, is the weaver who ties everything together."

155

22

LERA

I wake in a sweat. My sheets are damp, the memories of the dream still imprinted in my mind. *Shackles. Pain. A gray-skinned thing with too-long limbs and needle-sharp teeth inside a lipless maw.*

My heart races as I sit up, blinking into the darkness of my bedchamber. There are no shackles here. No monsters lurking in the shadows of this luxurious room, with its four-poster bed and finely carved dresser and pitcher of fresh water beside the washbasin. A dream, that's all it was. A nightmare. Like the nightmares I sometimes have about my old master, Zake, just different.

I swing my feet to the floor, the down comforter sliding off the bed with them. I consider picking it up but walk over and splash water on my face instead. The cool liquid beads on the pitcher's side, wetting my hands and shaking away the last of the nightmare. I sigh in relief, my mind once more mine. And normal.

Reaching inside me, I search for the magic I wielded healing Coal's back. There is nothing there. Not an empty well—just nothing. Stars take me. Something that is so real and potent one moment shouldn't be allowed to simply not exist the next. Maybe Autumn can explain—

A bolt of terror flashes through me, my heart leaping, the pitcher of water nearly falling from my hand just as the images come again. *My wrists burn, but I know worse is coming. A great, unbearable pain determined to make me howl—*

I gasp and stumble to my bed, feeling the silken sheets, the intruding nightmare gone with the same sudden efficiency as it came. Bloody damn stars. I rub my eyes with the heels of my hands. There is no pain. Not now, not waiting for me. However real the visions felt, they were not real.

They didn't even make sense, in retrospect. The *me* in my visions was determined to bear torment in silence, a point of pride that I little bothered with when Zake came after me. I had more important things to worry about at that point than whether I screamed.

I freeze, ice gripping my neck. I little cared about taking a beating in silence, but there's someone in this suite who cares about that very much. Whose past those images fit all too bloody well.

Coal. I pinch the bridge of my nose. My body has echoed River's magic, and Shade's. But Coal's? Coal's magic is different. Inside him. And now it's dragging me inside him too.

The milky pink eyes. The stench of decay. The promise of a lash —and worse.

Stumbling from my room, I walk down the short hallway and cross the common room to Coal's bedchamber, my bare feet tapping softly against the stone floor. No wonder he wanted the one isolated room. My shoulders tense, the evening chill peppering my nightshirt-clad skin with goosebumps.

If I'm right about the nightmares and what I think caused them, the Coal I'll find behind his closed door will be little happy to see me. Granted, I'm unlikely to have a better reception if I'm wrong.

Gathering my resolve, I knock. Softly at first, then louder. Then I give up the pointless exercise and push open the door.

"Coal?"

A dim room, a single lantern like a small star in the corner, augmenting the sliver of light from the moonless sky. Odd for Coal to have fallen asleep with a light on. Odder still that he is still sleeping, sprawled out shirtless on the bed, his blankets and pillows littering the floor like something out of Autumn's room.

I step toward the bed, my breath halting at the sight of Coal's spasming body, his face set in a silent scream that never escapes his lips. The male is dressed only in a pair of cotton trousers, his quivering chest covered in a thin sheen of sweat. His musky metallic scent fills the cold room. "Coal, wake up."

I touch his shoulder carefully, ready to jump away if he decides to kill first and wake up later. My hand comes away slick with sweat and blood from reopened gashes. There was only so much Shade's magic could do; it will take time for Coal's flesh to heal fully. If he gives it a chance to.

Coal gasps, drawing breath in slowing motions, as if bracing himself for something that is yet to come, his muscles straining against invisible binds. As if he's had this nightmare before. And his body knows what to expect next, knows the torment is only just starting. A thin trail of blood leaks from his mouth, where he's bitten his tongue or lip.

Kneeling on the mattress beside Coal, I shake him with all my strength, no longer caring whether he'll knock me across the room for it. "Coal! Wake up." My heart races, my hands changing tack to brush his face instead. His light hair, for once free from its bun, tangles around my fingers. "Coal. Open your eyes. It's me. Just me."

"Mortal?" Coal's confused growl is the most wonderful sound I've heard in a long time. The male's eyes open, wild and pale blue, surveying the room, the light, me. Bracing himself with his hands, Coal sits up roughly. "Why are you in my bed?"

"I had a nightmare." I swallow. "Your nightmare. I had your nightmare."

"What the bloody hell are you talking about?"

Right. He wasn't there for Autumn's explanation. Granted, I *was* there and I still little understand what's happening.

"The quint bond works differently with me—it lets me echo your magic. Sometimes. When we connect." I sigh. "I don't know. Ask Autumn. But that's why I could use River's earth magic in the arena and Shade's healing magic yesterday. And now, I'm seeing your dreams." I pause. Not just now. It's been happening since we first approached the Citadel.

"Go back to bed, mortal," Coal orders.

I don't budge, my heart speeding again. "There were shackles and pain, things with gray skin and pink eyes."

"The qoru," Coal says, pulling his hair back from his face, the movements stiff. The muscles of his arms and chest, so defined they would put a sculptor to shame, are coiled tightly beneath taut skin, and the heat radiating from him in waves brushes over my own flesh. "They are the dominant race in Mors. I'm unsure why you dreamt of them, but I don't imagine it was pleasant."

"It wasn't my dream, Coal." I find his eyes, glaring into his haunted blue gaze. "It was yours. And it wasn't the first one, either."

Coal says nothing, which I take as a good sign.

Rising to my knees, I slide close enough to lay a hand on one muscled shoulder. But for all the times Coal has helped me, I don't know how to offer comfort that the warrior will accept. "Shade and I worked hard on the flesh you are destroying again," I say, picking up a corner of the sheet to dab at Coal's back. "Are you in pain?"

"No."

I snort softly. "I truly don't know why I bother asking questions that I know you'll lie in response to."

A chuckle. Barely audible, but there.

I've never been so relieved to see a smile in my life.

Shaking my head, I brush my hand down his right shoulder, along the deadly curve of his bicep and forearm to the lacerated skin around his wrist. For the first time since I've touched him, I feel Coal tense beneath my fingers, a fine tremble running through his muscles. I touch his wrist lightly, like comforting a wild animal on the verge of bolting. With the damage to his back, no one looked twice at the marks the binds left behind when they bit into his skin today. Hearing Coal's breath still, I know I've found the source of the nightmares after all.

"You don't like being bound," I say softly.

"Do you?"

"I don't like the sound of a belt being pulled loose." I clench my jaw, needing a breath before I can think again. Coal's dream brushes against my memory, the dream and the shadow of Malikai's taunt. Beatings were the least of what Coal faced, I realize with a cold shiver. The qoru did to Coal the one thing Zake never did to me.

"I can't heal these," I caress the raw skin. "Not without Shade."

Coal pulls his hand out of my grip, all hints of humor gone. "I don't need to be healed." He catches my wrist when I reach for him again. "You should leave my bedchamber now, mortal. Whatever you imagined you felt has nothing to do with me."

"Oh, stars, are we back to the 'I've no notion of what you mean' horseshit?" I lean close enough to invade Coal's space, my heart pounding. A muscle ticks along his jaw. "And what *were* you dreaming of? Or do you imagine you were lying here peacefully when I came in?"

Coal's blue eyes pierce mine, his voice cold. "I dreamt of fucking. And not with you." I flinch and he releases me,

161

tossing my arm back into my lap. "Go to your own bed, mortal. Or to Shade's. Or to Tye's. Hell, go to River's bed. I little care so long as you are out of mine."

"You know what I think?" My words vibrate through the thick air. "I think you are telling the truth about little fearing a few lashes. It was being shackled that had you terrified. So damn scared, it gave you nightmares strong enough to bridge the bond with me. I think that even the notion of allowing someone to take hold of your wrists is more than you can bear without shaking. And you know what else?" I let the words hang for a heartbeat then lower my voice so low that only fae hearing could pick it up. "I think that what Malikai guessed happened to you in Mors is absolutely true."

This time, Coal doesn't order me out.

He gets up and leaves himself.

23

LERA

I pull on a pair of comfortable pants and a soft blue tunic, finding both by feel more than sight in the bedchamber's darkness. My mind spins through the sleepless fatigue, the sight of Coal storming out of the room burning in my memory. Have I made things worse, tearing open a half-healed wound? Should I stanch the damage by shutting the hell up now and giving the male the space he demands?

I discard that option even as it comes. Coal might have sold the whole damn quint on his not-caring act, but the stars will freeze and fall to the earth before I let him think I'm bowing quietly to the fiction. He's tried his way of coping for three hundred years. That's more than a fair stretch by anyone's measure. Especially mine.

My fingers make quick work of a braid, and I race into the common room—cursing as I trip over a gray lump of wolf that chooses this very moment to weave around my legs.

"Let me pass, Shade," I say, pushing him away—with little success. I growl softly. "I know you saw Coal pass through here five minutes ago. So are you protecting me from him or him from me? Because I can assure you that neither of those options will end well for you."

The wolf yips and gives me a guilt-inspiring look that he's no doubt spent centuries perfecting.

I cross my arms, glancing at the door. The five-minute lead Coal has on me is already stretching into ten, and the male knows the Citadel grounds far better than I do. "You know," I say, my voice light, "I wonder if your shifting magic might work on me as well. Want to stick around and try? What could possibly go wrong?"

With a small, highly displeased growl, Shade nips my hand and stalks away to curl himself in the corner, those mournful eyes watching me from atop fuzzy paws.

"I'm glad we agree," I tell the wolf sweetly, and I step out into the night, the cold air pricking my skin. Wrapping my arms around myself, I walk down the few steps from our door and blow out a slow breath. If it were me, I'd likely be making my way to a stable right now, wedging myself into a corner of an empty stall and letting the familiar scents of horse and hay calm my brittle nerves. What would be Coal's equivalent of my stable?

Almost immediately, my mind conjures an image in answer—wooden practice swords, a rope-wrapped post.

"He likely went to the training yard," a bright female voice says from the shadows, sending my heart into a gallop.

Heels grind against the gravel walkway as Klarissa's silhouette flows toward me. The material of her emerald gown is light enough to ripple in the breeze and clings to her body to show off perfect lines. A priceless diadem woven into her long, dark hair manages to catch what little light the night offers. "At least, I assume it's Coal you came out here to find? I'd check the training yard. You'll find it on the same side of the Citadel grounds as the practice arena, but farther north."

I swallow, my mouth dry. "Thank you, Elder." I bow, buying myself seconds to think, to hope that Shade might decide to follow me after all. Seconds pass but no help arrives. "You must forgive my startled reaction. I hardly expected a chance meeting outside my door at such an hour."

Klarissa tips her head back and laughs musically. "It's hardly a chance meeting, Leralynn. Well, meeting you is unexpected, but my personal curiosity has had me here for several hours now. I realize everything at the Citadel is new to you, but for me, having watched River's quint go through the trials once before, the differences this time around are too fascinating to overlook. You can't blame me for wondering whether today's regretful mishap in the dining hall might have had . . . more repercussions than were immediately obvious."

My fingers dig into my arms. "Of course, Elder. I'm certain keeping a watchful eye on all the trainees is one of your primary concerns."

"This is nothing like your males' first tour, you know," Klarissa says, gazing toward the arena. "Time was, River's quint was second in power only to the Elders Council itself. The raw power was there even in training. To surrender during a trial? Why, that would have been as unthinkable three centuries ago as finding Coal at the whipping post. Truth be told, I've never seen that male terrified before. Fear has a smell, you know. It's quite difficult to conceal, even with all the stoic bravado."

I nod and try to think of white dandelions—just in case thoughts have a smell too.

"I don't wish to detain you," Klarissa says, smiling so convincingly that a stranger might call it kind. "I simply saw you and thought it appropriate to admit firsthand to you that I was wrong. I confess that I believed the council should have pressed harder to sever you from the quint, but in retrospect, your presence here is one of the most valuable lessons for all of the Citadel. I imagine that after witnessing the destruction of such a powerful quint, none of the others in history will consider repeating the same mistakes. And we have you to thank for it."

I manage a bow before walking off, the night howling in my ears as I beg the stars not to find Coal in the training yard after all. That Klarissa doesn't know my quint as well as I do. Except of course she does.

I hear the clank of wood against targets and training posts before I get close enough to see a lone shirtless figure going through a deadly dance. Coal's blade is an extension of his muscled body, striking with preternatural speed as he battles phantoms, splintering wood and breaking bales of hay. Droplets of sweat and blood fly from him as he turns, the air whistling with the speed of his blade.

Settling on the sideline of the training yard, I pull my legs beneath me and watch, knowing better than to interrupt until Coal himself acknowledges my presence.

He doesn't. Not for an hour. Or two. Or four. He doesn't stop moving either, even as waves of sleep wash over me and I find myself dozing off. Each time I open my eyes, I find that nothing has changed but the time of night.

A hand touches my shoulder with the breaking dawn, and I find myself looking into Kora's concerned blue eyes.

"He's been here all night," I whisper.

Kora's brows rise as Coal chooses that moment to twist about and destroy one of the few remaining training posts with a single hard blow. "Good stars. Did he even feel the lashes?"

I want to laugh bitterly, which shows how tired I am. Is there anyone Coal doesn't have fooled except for Klarissa and me?

"Let's see if he's willing to share," Kora says, squeezing my shoulder as she rises. She makes a motion to her warriors, and the females all choose practice blades before walking onto the training yard at Kora's back. The female calls a friendly challenge to Coal, who nods without ever stopping and knocks two of the five females on their backsides before I can draw a breath.

"Human."

I jump at the sound of the familiar grating voice at my back. I turn slowly, finding Malikai behind a nearby tree. The male motions me over, his orange tunic billowing in the wind, outlining his tightly muscled chest and arms.

First Klarissa and now Malikai. And here I thought the

day couldn't get any worse. Malikai motions me over again, and my heart speeds with as much fear of approaching the bastard as disobeying his command. Straightening my spine, I rise to my feet and stride to him, my chin raised in a futile attempt to glare down my nose at the tall male. "What do you want, *sir*?"

Malikai leads us a few paces farther from the training yard, cutting off the line of sight to Coal and Kora, though I'm certain either would hear me if I screamed.

"Yes, we're still within earshot," Malikai confirms, following my gaze. His straight black hair is tied back in a thin ponytail, the long widow's peak stark against his tan face. Now that he's not trying to assault or humiliate me, I notice that his eyes are different colors—one a sky blue, the other a pale green. He shows me his empty palms then puts his hands into his pockets. "I don't imagine you're happy to see me."

"You would be right."

A corner of Malikai's mouth twitches, though with humor instead of cruelty. "At least we can speak plainly with each other—that's already a start."

I don't want to start anything with the bastard. "Excuse me, sir, my quint is waiting for me." I turn away from him.

"I needed to speak with you alone, Leralynn," Malikai says to my back. "I realize you've little reason to like me right now, but will you at least hear me out? I need your help."

I spin angrily. "Unless I can help you drop dead, I'm not interested in aiding anything you do."

He sighs, his lips pressing together. "Listen, before you

burn bridges you may wish to make use of. I'm a bastard, but I'm not an idiot—I've no notion of why River surrendered during the trial, but I know he could have knocked us all into the Gloom with half a thought."

"You mean the trial where you went after me instead of the flag?" I say.

"Yes, the trial where I went after the weakest link to avoid the appearance of giving anything but my utmost effort. Had I done any less, my whole quint would have found itself having much the same experience as Coal did last night, so you'll forgive me for choosing them over you."

I cross my arms, which Malikai takes as an invitation to return to his original point.

"Given the other things that have happened since then, I'm not eager to face either River or Coal again in a trial. I need you to request your second trial. Right now."

"Did I do something to make you think I'm suicidal?" I say in what I think an extremely reasonable tone under the circumstances.

The corner of Malikai's mouth twitches again. "You will request the Individual Trial, face me, make a show of putting up a fight—forget a show, you can fight as much as you please—and then you'll surrender. You can still take the trial over, but the council won't pit our quints against each other for a third time. I will promise not to hurt you. I'll even let you land a few blows." He spreads his arms. "Your quint never has to see mine again and vice versa. A neat and clean solution that lets us both walk away unscathed."

"This sounds like a command decision, sir," I say. "You should discuss it with River."

Malikai grabs my wrist, making me gasp. "I caused a great many problems for River yesterday. If I were him, I'd agree and then change the order of combat at the last moment. I can't risk facing Coal in the arena. Quint trainees *die* in trials, Leralynn. I won't let that happen to me."

"Maybe you should have considered that yesterday," I say.

Malikai's lips tighten. "I made a mistake. It was a spur-of-the-moment foolery that I can't undo. Or do you imagine that if I simply go apologize, we can all put this behind us?"

A grunt of pain sounds from the arena. Coal destroying warriors, one after the other.

I pull my hand free of Malikai's grip and stifle the urge to wipe my wrist against my uniform. "No, I don't imagine an apology will suffice," I agree. "Nor do I think I want to make your life easier, sir. Excuse me."

"Don't you understand—"

"You asked me to put on a show to ensure that you never have to face Coal in the arena. I said no. And now, sir, I'm telling you to go to hell."

"I'd consider the consequences of that, if I were you." Malikai steps closer, his nostrils flaring as he takes in my scent. He smiles, showing sharp canines, and his voice lowers. "Deny me now, and I'll make yesterday's dinner experience a nightly occurrence. You see, Leralynn, your males have a weakness the size of a barn door—they are bloody easy to provoke. What do you imagine your wolf shifter will do if I, say, slap your ass right under his nose? We already know how to get Coal's blood boiling over his common sense. A bit of prodding and I'll have River and

Tye worked over just as easily. Refuse me now, and my quint and I will ensure there is blood watering the whipping post grounds every evening you're here. It will be a sight to see."

My breath stills, my muscles rigid. "You're mad," I whisper to the male. "You are talking about walking through a hayloft with an open flame, just to see how many bales you can destroy before the whole barn crashes on your ears."

Malikai shakes his head. "I'm not mad. I'm desperate. When your alternative is being burned at the stake, treading hay with an open flame starts sounding quite attractive."

24

LERA

J do as Malikai says, heading directly to the council to request the trial. To ensure that my fight will come first. My heart pounds, my squeezing lungs barely letting me form the words. I hate doing this, hate keeping it from the others. I hate that I have to.

"I'll make the arrangements," Klarissa tells me, a small smile curving her painted lips as she walks me from the foyer of the Elders Council tower. "Make your way to the trial arena. You'll find a clean uniform in the preparation room. Your quint will meet you there. I'll make certain of that personally."

This last part sends an arrow of dread through me, its point sharp enough to nick my heart.

A quarter hour later, my black pants are buttoned and my shaking fingers are attempting to tie the sash around my burgundy tunic when the door to the preparation room slams open.

A sword falls from its hook on the wall, the ring of steel on stone echoing from the high ceiling.

For a moment, Coal's blue eyes are all I see.

"What did you do?" he roars, his hot hands pinning my ribcage against the wall while my feet dangle in the air, my hair loose and wild around my shoulders. His pulse thunders so hard, I can see it against his neck. His metallic scent fills my lungs.

A lupine growl fills the room in answer to Coal's question, the sound guttural and laden with the promise of death and dismemberment.

"Do that one more time and I'll muzzle you, dog," Coal snaps over his shoulder.

Bloody stars. This reaction alone proves Malikai right. The males are too easy to provoke. I sigh and meet Coal's sapphire-blue eyes, forcing my voice to a calm lightness as I explain Malikai's ultimatum.

Coal's eyes widen, his mouth opening, then closing— whether in rage or disbelief, it's too hard to say.

"Which part specifically did you find confusing?" I say finally, my legs still dangling above the ground. I think the male actually forgot he was holding me up. "If you let me down, I'll draw a picture."

Coal drops me and sinks into a chair.

"Don't lean back," I say. "Your wounds have opened, and those chairs look expensive."

Coal's eyes flash.

Tye snorts.

"I hate to say this"—Autumn helps herself to a glass of dry wine, the presence of which, I'm learning, is one advantage of having Tye along anywhere—"but Malikai is a smart little bastard. The only certain way for him to avoid facing you four in the arena is to face Lera. And the only way to make certain Lera's match happens first is to have her call for it."

"What if Malikai hurts her?" Tye says.

"If he wanted to murder me, he could have snapped my neck this morning when we were alone," I say. "I really believe it's not my death he's after, but rather a lack of his own."

"Plus, the arena's holding wards will engage the moment Lera utters 'surrender.'" Autumn flicks a thin blond braid behind her back. "Fortunately, that part is not left to the levelheaded honor of hot-blooded warriors."

"Stop trying to make the mortal's bullheaded bravery sound reasonable," Coal tells Autumn. He picks up a wineglass but it shatters in his grip before he manages to drink. "Giving in to Malikai's demands will not make the bastard more considerate, any more than feeding a crocodile will make it more docile."

"And escalating this tit-for-tat will do no one any favors either," I tell Coal. "Point is, the cost of surrender is acceptable. As with the first trial, we will retake this later with a different quint. Malikai wants out of this mess. And frankly, so do I."

Coal growls and moves to lean against the far wall.

"*Point is,*" River says with a commander's bloody calm,

"Leralynn has already requested the trial and Klarissa has accepted."

Silence follows his words and I realize I've avoided looking at River until now. I was right to. His gray eyes are a storm as they seize mine, his beautiful, high cheekbones tight. Whatever my intent, I've flouted his authority entirely. There are very few ways to hurt River more.

He clears his throat. "Hence, less arguing and more getting ready, please." He straightens and clasps his hands behind his back, frowning at the door to the arena. "Leralynn, once you are in there, you will be unable to see or hear us, but we will be watching you from above. Remember that no one can hear you or Malikai either. The wards will pick up on the surrender announcement, but that is it. Do you understand?"

I nod.

"Similarly to the Quint Trial, the Individual Trial can end one of three ways," River says. "Someone is rendered unconscious, which means victory for the warrior left standing. Surrender, which means the whole trial must start over against a different quint. Or death."

"This works in your favor, Lera," Autumn chimes in. "Malikai can't risk striking you so hard as to make you lose consciousness. Then *he* would win, but the trial itself would continue, which would mean the rest of his quint would face the rest of yours. He won't risk giving Coal, or any of these murderous idiots"—she gestures around the room—"a chance to kill one of them."

"Don't get brave in there, Lilac Girl," Tye says, twisting me toward him, his broad shoulders suddenly blocking out the entire room. "It's a game, and take it from one who has cheated at a great many games, the last thing you want to do is make things more complex than they must be."

Before I can reply, Tye's green eyes sink into mine, the humor in them fading to something more primal. His hands brush my ears, tucking the thick strands of hair away from my face, before he leans down to brush his lips over mine in a possessive caress. My mouth tingles as he pulls away, his nose hesitating in my hair to draw in a lungful of my scent. "Promise you won't be brave."

I put my hands on either side of Tye's face. His skin is clean-shaven and smooth to the touch, even as the tight muscles beneath his jaw shift to relieve the grinding tension. "I won't do anything brave," I promise, injecting my words with as much confidence as I can muster. "The greatest threat I face is surrendering so quickly that the whole Citadel realizes the farce—but I imagine that Malikai will make things look believable enough for the first few minutes. So don't worry."

"I can't—"

I lean forward and brush my lips over his a final time. "I said, don't worry."

Shade steps up to me next, his golden eyes sharp as he runs his fingers through my hair, reaching back to gather the whole lot of it into a tight braid. "We'll be standing right beside Malikai's quint—he knows who will pay the price if he tries something. So, nice and easy. You are too brave for your own good, cub, but we need that bravery for another day." Leaning down, he presses a kiss against my forehead, slips his face toward my ear, and—

I yelp, rubbing the top of my earlobe, which now has a drop of blood on it. "What was that?"

Shade grins. "My scent. Very much on you. I want that bastard to remember exactly whose mate he is facing across the sand."

A small smile touches my lips and I turn to Coal. "Are you planning on biting me as well?"

"No." Pushing away from the wall, Coal strides to me with hard steps. He grips my shoulders, his blue eyes flaming. "If something goes wrong, mortal, kill the bastard. No pulling blows."

My senses fill with his musky scent, his anger, his need. It's all I can do to give him a small nod.

"I think you missed the part about this being a game," Tye says from the side.

"There are no games," Coal snaps without breaking eye contact with me. "Not when it matters. And this matters. If you need to kill him, you do it. Understand?"

"And you have some way for me to accomplish this?" I ask.

Coal taps my chest. "You do. Don't forget it."

The sound of a gong breaks apart our little gathering, and with a final check of a dulled sword that Coal settles into my hands, I step out onto the sand of the trial arena for the second time.

Like before, sand stretches in every direction, the sun beating down into my eyes. I wonder if there is always sun in the arena, another trick of magic ensuring that every trainee experiences the same environment as the other. Squinting against the brightness, I stride toward the center, which is a bit of a feat—my body is all but trembling despite what I told the males.

Warriors die in this arena. And I can't be one of them.

I surrender, I want to shout to the winds. But I can't. Not yet. So I take step after step until Malikai's form appears before me. He's dressed in the orange tunic of his quint, his eyes nearly translucent in the sunlight. His gaze meets mine, for once steady instead of cruel—almost calming.

"You are all right," he says quietly. "You made the right choice."

I shift my sword, my eyes darting toward the sky.

"They can't hear us," Malikai reminds me. "They will only hear the surrender because it will trigger a ward. It is safe to speak if you wish, but there isn't much time."

The second gong sounds and Klarissa announces the start of the trial.

Malikai draws his sword in a single motion, closing the distance to me so quickly that I yelp in surprise.

"Block the bloody attack," he yells, slowing his sword just enough for me to remember what I'm supposed to be doing and bring up my blade. He scowls. "Pay attention. I can't do this dance for both of us alone. Block low."

I drop my sword just as Malikai takes a glorious swing. It hits the center of my blade in such a way that I actually manage to maintain my balance. Coal's training rushes into my mind, moving too quickly for me to make much use of it. Gripping the sword with two hands, I swing wildly with all my might, which effectively turns me in a circle when Malikai slides out of the way.

He circles me now, a cat playing with a mouse as his

blade jets in and out, the dull blade slicing across my ankles and belly and shoulder. Unlike Coal's blows in training, Malikai's slices don't hurt and certainly don't threaten to break my bones. My heart slows enough to look around and watch what I'm doing, my blocks coming faster and more effective. Low block, step right, slide out of the way and swing for Malikai's head, only to drop the tip of my blade to parry a cut aimed at my midsection.

"So those bastards did manage to teach a human something," Malikai says, the hint of approval in his voice somehow cheering me. "It's almost time for you to surrender, but I promised you could land a handful of blows. Take your pick."

Kill him, Coal's voice says in my head. I snort at the silliness of it and swing for Malikai's flank instead. His arm drops in a perfect parry that manages to miss my blade by a hair, and he grunts with approval.

"Not bad," he says. "I'll give you one more."

"I don't want it," I tell the male, my heart pounding hard from the exertion. I realize the truth of my words as I say them. I don't want to strike someone who isn't defending himself, who is no true threat to me. Malikai might get pleasure from such things, but I do not. "I need nothing more from you but the promise that you will not go near me or my quint ever again."

"You have it," Malikai says smoothly, closing the distance to bring the dulled edge of his blade against my throat. "Now surrender and let's end this."

"I surrender!" I yell, Malikai and I both freezing as we wait for the gong to end the battle.

Nothing.

No gong. No thickened air. No disembodied voice. As if no one heard.

"Say it again," Malikai says, circling me with his blade out. "The wards will pick up the word. Say it again."

"I surrender!" I yell, throwing my head back and squinting at the sun.

Nothing. My heart quickens, my eyes finding Malikai's equally confused stare. I throw my sword down and hold up my hands, shouting as loud as my burning lungs will allow. "I surrender! End the trial! I yield!"

Malikai's jaw tightens. "It appears surrender isn't an option in this trial today. My apologies, human, but death it will have to be."

"You can win without killing me," I protest, moving away from Malikai, my hands raised in the air. "Knock me down, draw blood, whatever it is that tells the arena the battle is over."

Malikai shakes his head. "I'd love to help you, I truly would. But not with those four immortals looking down at us like wolves who smell blood. The only way I am walking out of the Citadel alive is if their quint is so broken, they have no energy to spare for the likes of me. My life against yours. There isn't much question as to which option I choose."

25

COAL

Coal crouched at the top of the bowl that was the arena, looking at Malikai and Lera circling each other below. Her slim, precious form against Malikai's towering muscle. Strands of auburn hair that had fallen loose from her braid whipped about her face in the arena's preternatural wind.

Coal's jaw tightened. The mortal was faltering, her movements too tentative and exploratory for true combat. Once Lera made it out of this tangle in one piece, Coal would have some lengthy conversation with her about when exactly the fight starts.

At least Malikai was true to his word. With his trained eye, Coal could see the male's show, the game he was putting on for the Citadel. No one truly expected the girl to do much, and the cat-and-mouse game he was leading her on was as good a diversion as any.

Coal's breath halted for a moment as Malikai lowered his guard and Lera missed her chance—didn't make the kill strike like he'd told her to. It was too late to worry on that score, though, as Malikai was already moving and holding the blade to her throat. And then—

Silence. There was nothing more coming from the bowl than there'd been earlier.

Lera threw back her head.

Nothing. Coal twisted to River, whose own eyes were a wide, stormy gray.

Down below, the mortal had tossed down her weapon, holding up her hands.

"Leralynn surrenders," River bellowed across the arena, his voice reaching to the stars themselves. "Stop the trial."

"You can't surrender on her behalf," Autumn said gently, her voice hitching. "The Arena won't allow it. It's the ward. Someone tampered with the ward to keep it from triggering."

Light flashed beside Coal and suddenly Shade was in his wolf form, growling his defiance to the world. The wolf's golden eyes fixed on the girl below, his body shifting his weight to his hind legs as—

"Shade, no!" Coal bellowed, but it was too late.

The animal leapt into the air, which *looked* to be the only obstacle between them and the trial below. But that was an illusion. It wasn't air between them and Lera at all. It was magic. A fierce, violent magic, as old as time itself.

Coal's breath stopped as Shade's paws hit the invisible shield that those magical wards had erected to keep away interference. A sound like a mosquito sizzling against a lantern sounded for a heartbeat, and then a flood of magic rushed over the wolf's body.

Shade's howl pierced the air, his body twitching uncontrollably.

Gritting his teeth, Coal extended himself over the arena's invisible ceiling to haul Shade back onto the viewing platform. Pain exploded along Coal's arms, the magic extracting its punishment for daring to interfere with the proceedings. The shocks ran through his spine, searing his muscles, arching his already bleeding back.

Down below, Lera's body spasmed too, her back arching so oddly and suddenly that even Malikai seemed taken aback.

Hauling the unconscious wolf onto the platform, Coal crouched, his breath heaving as he watched the horror unfolding below. He rarely felt true fear anymore, not when he was awake. But now, seeing Lera a hairbreadth from losing her life, Coal's heart raced so quickly, he could barely think.

Down below, the mortal's left arm twitched.

Coal's gaze cut to his own limb. The elbow that had been in direct contact with the wards the longest was still spasming like a deranged snake.

"Lera used my magic during the first trial," River said, grabbing Autumn's attention. "If I rupture the damn earth from here to the far wall—"

"You were within arm's reach during the trial," Autumn said, shaking her head. "And Shade was flush against her yesterday. Given your failure with her in the practice arena,

I'm confident that both strength of magic and proximity are required."

Coal's chest tightened. "Not with me," he heard himself say, already rising to his feet. His heart thundered but he turned to the petite female. "She can feel me at a distance."

Autumn's brow creased. "I don't understand."

Coal's fists tightened. "She can feel me at a distance. When I'm in . . . distress, she knows. As if my fears penetrate into her. I just saw it—she flinched when I reached over the barrier and reacted again to the shocks in my arm. It's my magic she's latching on to, isn't it?"

Autumn nodded slowly, her intelligent eyes sorting through information. "Your magic, unlike River's, is turned inward. So, yes, if Lera is somehow connecting with you through your fear, then she may be brushing against your magic while she is there. Reacting to it."

Coal swallowed. "If she can taste my fear when I'm trying very hard to block it, then would my surrendering to it strengthen Lera's connection to me? Give her better access to my magic?"

"It is possible," Autumn admitted.

Possible. That was enough. Coal turned to River, gripping the commander's wide eyes. "I need you to trigger every bloody memory I have of Mors," Coal said, holding out his wrists as his heart pounded. "Bind me and give no quarter. And then . . . and then don't let me bloody kill you, because I'm going to fight like hell itself."

LERA

I'm unarmed, unable to surrender, and trapped with an immortal warrior who believes the only solution to his current problem lies in ending my life. My eyes flick to the top of the arena, where the blinding sun blocks my view of the spectators. But I know my males are there. Watching. Knowing that I'm trying.

Malikai comes at me with his dull sword raised, his hard face set with the determination of a farmer catching livestock for dinner. No anger, no regret, no emotion at all besides an ironclad certainty that in a moment I'll be dead. The weapon in his hand is nearly as big as I am, his large hands powerful enough to snap me in two.

I dive to the ground. The sand meets me, rising into the air and filling my mouth as I roll over my right shoulder and get to my feet on Malikai's other side. My breath quickens, my muscles tight and quivering. I wipe my forearm across my face, spitting out sand.

The male snarls, his previously emotionless eyes now flashing with excitement, like a predator who's caught the first scent of prey. Bloody stars. Throwing the sword aside, Malikai lunges for me, and this time there is no escape as he pins my back to the ground, his powerful thighs straddling my heaving sides.

I buck beneath him, digging my shoulders into the sand as I struggle to make space and slither free. Malikai's weight is a stone atop me, making each breath a hard-fought chore. Unable to buck the male off, I curl my hand into a fist and swing at his nose.

Which I know Coal said is stupid, but I don't remember why.

I have my answer in the next heartbeat as Malikai catches my arm easily and barks a laugh. Fishing for my other wrist, the male transfers both to one steel fist. "Might as well put on a show, don't you think?" he tells me, his white canines flashing in the sunlight. Before I can respond, Malikai's hips lift for a moment of breath-permitting bliss as he twists my trapped wrists, forcing me to roll. To turn face-down in the sand. Then his weight settles back atop me. "Your males are watching, you know. What do you think they are making of this?" He laughs, stretching my trapped wrists out above my head.

"Is this the bull?" a voice echoes in the darkness of a stone dungeon. "The one you can't seem to tame?" I know that voice. Just as I know that after today, it will never speak again.

My face is in the sand. I can't move. Can't breathe.

Can't scream. Malikai's weight holds me in place, squeezing away what little air I manage to gulp around mouthfuls of sand. Fear, cold and hard, rushes through me, spurring my heart into a blinding gallop. Above me, Malikai shifts again and something hard, like his knee or shin, presses painfully into my ribs. The bones shift and bend and howl beneath the growing pressure.

My mind goes blank, everything I've learned disappearing into a fog of pure panic and instinct. I pull against my hands, buck, scream—

The stone is cold and hard beneath my knees, my binds trapping me to the wall as the qoru approaches, its gray skin matte in the gloom. The folds that pass for its nose compress together as it snorts and opens a maw of sharp teeth to speak. "It doesn't look all that strong to me."

"Be careful." The second qoru comes closer, his stench filling my nose.

"Which of them do you think will scream the loudest when your ribs snap into your heart?" Malikai muses, leaning down to whisper into my ear. "My money would usually be on the mate, but he'll likely cower into his wolf and stay there for another century or two. River . . . No, that one likes to put on airs. I truly hope it's the Mors whore who—"

My elbow moves, breaking the bonds holding me in place to plunge into the horrid fold of flesh passing for the qoru's nose. Power flows through my body, pulsing with my heart, filling my muscles with blood and strength.

The qoru screams.

Malikai screams as my elbow smashes into his face. There's a cracking sound and warm liquid soaks the arm of my tunic. The weight on my back lightens, but I'm already pulling my other hand from Malikai's grasp. Power surges inside me, filling my muscles with heat.

Filling me with hot, blinding rage.

Blood. Enemy blood. The smell of it makes my heart pound with excitement. My nostrils flare, scenting my adversary's sudden weakness. His close, sweet death. The blood coursing through my veins simmers, each organ it touches lighting with new strength. My lungs fill with all the air in the world, my eyes seeing so clearly that I can count the sand grains beneath my face.

I throw Malikai off me easily, his heavy body sending a cloud of sand into the air as it lands. Blood still flowing from his broken nose seeps into the sand.

"What are you?" Malikai screams, his pale, mismatched eyes wide, his hands in the air to ward off my approach. The vein on the side of his neck pulses, beads of sweat trailing from the raven widow's peak in the middle of his forehead. He is afraid. Terrified. I can smell it.

And I love it.

Dropping to one knee, I sink my fist into Malikai's stomach, the muscled flesh hard beneath my knuckles.

"I surrender!" Malikai hollers to the arena.

But the arena doesn't care.

"My quint," Malikai calls to me, slithering away. His words are muffled, his breath coming in gasps. "Please. You know what a death does to a quint." His hands drop, his head rising to expose his bare neck to me. "I surrender," he whispers. "I won't fight."

My fist tightens, my pulse a pounding drum, the *lub-dub*,

lub-dub, *lub-dub* echoing through my head. Waves of pain and humiliation wash over me again and again as I cock my fist to put an end to this qoru's existence. It's not worth calling it life.

Power flares in my blood.

Stop. The command comes from everywhere inside me, in a voice that is mine and not mine. *You are Lera.*

I pull my strike as it flies, neatly knocking Malikai unconscious.

27

LERA

"I do like that dress," Tye says, leaning in the open door of my bedchamber—which I'm sure I closed and locked before starting to change. His sharp face is split into a wide, glinting smile, his white tunic unbuttoned to the deep carve of his sternum.

I grip the sides of the gown before it can fall to my ankles. "How did you get in here?"

Tye blinks, his brilliant green eyes wide with innocence. "The same way I've gotten into most places for a few centuries. Good thing, too—you look in need of some assistance, lass."

I scowl down at the fabric, which, in addition to being a gorgeous sapphire-blue satin, is also voluminous and unwieldy enough to make me consider going to the dining hall in my undershorts. Not that I want to go to a celebratory dinner of any kind just now, but that's my problem, not Tye's. Or the dress's. I sigh. The bodice is an open-backed thing that is supposed to lace up around my ribs. It's the same one I wore to meet with the Elders Council, and somehow, I still cannot figure out how to put it on. It was hard enough then; now, with my shaking and depleted muscles, it's impossible. I'm certain the tailor cackled himself silly after making it. "If you can work out how to attach this thing to me, I won't ask after the lock," I concede to Tye, turning my back to him.

The door clicks closed and the male's measured footsteps approach me from behind. His thick arms wrap around my waist as his scent of pine and citrus fills my lungs. The heat from Tye's body seeps into me, sending shivers across my skin. And doing nothing for the bloody dress.

"You were going to help with the bodice," I say over my shoulder.

"No, I wasn't," Tye says into my ear, his warm breath its own caress that makes me want to melt into his body and pull away at the same time.

I fight against the latter, keeping my chin raised high, like the other males did in the aftermath of the trial only hours ago. We won. Passed the Individual Trial. Secured the victory. I, through beating Malikai; the others by virtue of Malikai's entire quint yielding before the other four fights could even begin, too afraid of the malfunctioning surrender ward to step into the arena with my males.

It doesn't matter what my victory cost. That I came within a breath of killing. That Coal's eyes were blank by the time I made it to him, the shadows underneath so deep he looked bruised. That Shade's wolf had only just stopped whimpering and regained enough consciousness to shift back into fae form. My chest squeezes painfully at the memory of his sweat-drenched body curled up on the stone, flinching away from me when I tried to comfort him— which was an improvement on him being unable to move at all.

What matters is that there is now one less rune on everyone's neck, and we are having dinner with Autumn and Kora's quint in the dining hall to celebrate.

I force the expected normalcy into my voice. "You are the one who came to offer help, if I recall."

"Aye. But I wasn't talking about the dress." Tye's arms tighten, his large body folding protectively around me. The hard muscles of his thighs and abdomen press into my flesh. "Stop pretending, Lilac Girl," Tye purrs. "See, lying is a skill. An art. Of which I consider myself a seasoned master. You . . . Well, you don't even reach novice rank on that particular front."

"I'm not sure—"

"The trial." Tye turns me toward him, the dress abandoned to fall into a pool of blue on the floor. His thumbs trace the length of my cheekbones, his stunning face so close to mine, I can see that smattering of freckles on one cheek, feel his skin's heat. "Talk to me, lass."

I swallow, an involuntary chill running down my spine. "We are a warrior quint destined to fight the terrors of Mors," I say in a voice too even to be mine. "Today's fight ended in victory. End of discussion and time to eat."

"Now, that sounds very much like Coal," Tye says.

I sigh, my shoulders falling. "It sounds like Coal because it is from Coal. I tried to ask him about—"

"Well, that was your first mistake," Tye interrupts, his face lowering toward mine. "You were talking to the wrong male. It truly is better never to talk to Coal. Especially not when you could be doing this instead." Tye's hands tighten on either side of my face, tipping it up as his warm, velvety lips brush over mine with unexpected gentleness.

My heart speeds in spite of itself, my body aching for more, even while my mind still grips the stoicism I thought I was doing a good job of portraying. The safety of Tye's broad shoulders and corded arms wraps around me, his heat and scent drowning out the world with no effort at all. For once, after hours of holding myself in check, I want to give in, let go. Tye, with his quick hands and quicker smile, is the easiest male to sink into and forget that anything else exists. My hands reach for him without my permission, my palms resting on the hard edges of his pectorals. Tye's heartbeat, vibrating through layers of trained, hardened muscle, is a soft *lub, lub, lub* against my touch.

Tye's hands slip from my face down to my hips, the calloused skin scraping wonderfully along my body. Gripping my waist, he lifts me easily into the air and sets me atop my high bed. "You know," he says, kneeling on the mattress and straddling my thighs as my hands stretch back to brace myself, "many consider combat to be a strong aphrodisiac."

My pulse pounds. "I'm not one of them," I say, even as my nipples peak and moisture pools between my legs, my body's own arousal betraying me. My raspy voice makes me cringe. Stars. It's wrong how badly my body wants Tye's lips, Tye's body, the pleasures that the male knows so well how to offer. All the things that I deserve none of. "Stop," I whisper, wanting him to do anything but.

Tye raises a brow, two fingers touching the underside of my chin. His nostrils flare delicately, tasting my scent. "Tell me why."

I can't.

He tips his head, his red hair swinging. "Do you deserve punishment instead of a reward?" His mouth pulls into a feral grin, his canines glistening in the setting sun. "I think something can be arranged."

"That's not what I said, Tye." I gasp as the male takes hold of my hips and moves me further onto the four-poster bed, all while turning my chest wrap and undershorts into little more than shredded and discarded rags. Cool air tickles my exposed skin. I press my legs together, only to discover Tye's knee perfectly blocking my way.

I reach between his legs, suddenly desperate to wrap my fingers around him, to make him feel what I'm feeling. He grips my wrist, something flickering in his eyes. I move my other hand and he stops it just as quickly, holding my wrists at my sides.

I frown. "Tye—"

"Uh-uh, lass. Not today." His voice is a rod of steel covered in thick velvet, his eyes unreadable. Leaning low, his lips trace a line from my navel to my sternum to my neck. "Punishment," he whispers, his hands brushing along my arms, extending them over my head. "You don't get to move."

Moisture slicks my thighs and slithers down to the coverlet beneath.

Tye's nostrils puff and he smiles approvingly, making my skin heat. Snatching the remains of my chest wrap, he wraps the cloth deftly around my wrists, attaching the end to a bedpost and making my eyes widen.

"You aren't Coal, lass," he whispers into my ear. "You are Lera. And you are entitled to your own sensations. Your own memories." His eyes on me, warm moss in the golden light, he shifts his mouth to cover my nipple, biting it just hard enough to send a glorious sting through my breast. I gasp softly and he moves to the other nipple. "Stay still," he says. Watching my face, he bites again, harder this time.

My body tightens inexplicably, the spark of pain nothing compared to the sudden gripping need that takes my sex. I moan softly before I can help it.

"Good lass." Tye's tongue replaces his teeth, leisurely circling around the sore spot before lapping at it gently, sending a streak of fire through my core. He sits up on his knees, his wide palms brushing my naked flesh in long, luxurious strokes that move closer and closer to my core with each pass. He slows as he reaches my inner thighs, nodding approvingly at the wetness as he presses my thighs further apart still, exposing my increasingly throbbing sex to his mercy.

"Now that I have your full attention," Tye says softly, stroking his thumb once through my slit and casually flicking his nail against the bud in a way that makes my buttocks quiver, "let us discuss the virtues of pretending to feel nothing because someone tells you to."

I open my mouth to reply, but Tye's fingers trace a predatory circle around my opening and I whimper instead, pulling against the cloth.

"Get ready to not feel, Lilac Girl."

I close my eyes as his head descends between my legs, his breath ruffling my coiled auburn locks, the thin stream of air turning hot enough to awaken each of my nerves. Having thoroughly ruffled the hair, the stream creeps closer to my slit, the promise of heat on moist, tender flesh making my heart pound. "You . . . are using . . . magic," I manage to say. "That's not fair."

"I'm a thief," Tye says, his all-but-steaming breath prickling the inside of my sex, stoking my desire. "I don't do fair."

No. Clearly not.

The next touch of Tye's magic has me writhing, the flame inside my sex spreading through my body in growing desperation. I bite my lips, my hands curling around the coverlet. Just as I think my mastery over myself is assured, however, Tye's tongue begins to lap at me, a tiger playing with his meal. I arch toward him, my apex begging for attention.

Tye grips my thighs, my bucking, squirming hips no match for his strong arms. A sharp, delicious prickle of pain spreads from just inside my sex, sending my fingernails into my palms. "What was that?"

His head rises, his tongue sliding over his canines. "I warned you not to move," he says, the wicked twinkle in his eyes as bright as the sun. "Now, quiet. I'm busy."

The lapping returns, interrupted by occasional long

strokes of his tongue and gentle scrapes of his teeth that make me buck like a wild horse. When I return to soft whimpering after another of those maneuvers, I realize a low rumbling sound has filled the air, coming not from Tye's mouth but—

"Are you purring?" I ask.

Tye flushes, spreading my sex with renewed vigor as he finally stokes my apex. My question is forgotten as a shudder rakes my body.

I feel as though I'm on a cliff's edge, one hairbreadth away from falling into an oblivion of agony and bliss.

"How is that *not* feeling treating you, lass?" Tye says, having mercy a moment later by plunging his finger into my opening and freeing my release with the force of an arrow.

I fall over the cliff, the binds on my arms burning to ash beneath Tye's magic, my body screaming with exhausted pleasure. When I collapse, I'm in Tye's arms, which have somehow moved to cradle me in his lap.

When I can breathe again, I snake my hands under his shirt, my fingertips tracing his muscles and heading lower. Tye's breath catches, the hardness beneath me a newly living, throbbing thing. I wriggle, turning in his lap to face him as my hands brush that bulge, seeking the laces holding his breeches in place. I lick my lips, knowing Tye's eyes follow the tip of my tongue. "I want to taste you," I whisper. "I want to know whether you taste better than chocolate."

The flash of hurt in Tye's eyes is so quick that I'm uncertain I truly saw it before he grins, waggling his brows. "Oh, I'm much, *much* better than chocolate."

I wrap the tail of his fly's lace around my finger, but Tye's hand closes over mine before I can let him loose.

"I'm so much better than chocolate that dinner will taste bland," he drawls. "I can't do that to you. It would just be cruel."

I open my mouth to protest, but Tye gathers me to him again, his calloused hand rubbing circles on my back as he buries his face in my hair, breathing deeply and throbbing beneath me.

Tye. *Tye.* The male I'd considered the most easygoing of the quint may be the most challenging puzzle yet.

28

LERA

"*A* toast," Kora says, lifting her wine goblet into the air and grinning at our two quints and Autumn, all sitting around the dinner table. Well, mostly sitting, given that Shade, Coal, and I can barely keep ourselves upright. Even now, the wolf shifter's yellow eyes are dull and filled with pain. Kora swallows, her voice faltering for a moment before regaining its hard-won cheerfulness. "To the only quint in Citadel history to pass a second trial before the first."

"That isn't technically correct," Autumn says. "Fifty years ago—"

"Quiet, Sparkle." Tye lifts his glass, the dark red wine in it releasing aromas of black currant and vanilla. "Details of history are no reason to let a drinking opportunity pass us by."

I take a small sip. The wine's full flavor and velvety

texture spread over my tongue. Stars, but it's good, especially beside the thick slices of roast lamb and aged cheese that weigh down the table and make my stomach dance.

As if smelling my thoughts, River pulls my chair closer to his with one arm and pushes my plate closer to me, adding a sauce to the garlic-baked lamb in the center. "Eat," he says. "You need to eat more."

I wince. "I'm not too sure of that."

"Well, *I* need you to eat more." River's eyes roam my skin. "Would you like more carrots? They're good for you. The cheese too, if—"

"You will make an excellent grandmother one day," I tell the prince of Slait, taking a bite of aged cheese just to make him stop fussing. The moment the slice leaves my plate, a new one appears. Together with a helping of grapes. I roll my eyes at River, using the motion as an excuse to glance over at Coal, who has barely looked at me since the trial.

He suddenly finds his food endlessly fascinating.

Right. I clear my throat. "Has anyone seen Malikai?"

"Not since the council ordered his quint to the tower," Kora says. "Apparently, they were none too pleased that four of the five quint warriors yielded before the combat started. They're bastards, yes, but I little envy them just now." She winces, either in empathy for Malikai or at her newfound imprudence at speaking so plainly of the council.

I pick up my knife and fork and slice into the lamb, which releases a bouquet of tingling spices. "What will happen to them?"

"They'll live another day," Coal says, finishing his wine

in a single long gulp. His loose black shirt is open at the collar to reveal a muscled neck and still-pale skin. "Which would not have been the case if they'd stepped onto the sand with the surrender ward disabled," he continues casually, violence edging his words.

"A most unusual situation," says a musical voice that makes my throat burn.

Everyone at the table rises to their feet, bowing to Klarissa and Elidyr as they stride up to our table. Well, Elidyr strides; Klarissa flows with a dancer's grace. The female is dressed in a satin gown the color of onyx, and she owns every inch of the shimmering fabric. A fine gold chain woven into her dark hair hangs down onto her forehead, the tear-shaped diamond at its center giving the impression of a third eye.

"Oh, I like that," Tye says, his eyes sparking at Klarissa's jewel. "You wouldn't wish to part with it for a tidy—"

I hit him in the solar plexus.

"*Oof.*" Tye rubs his sternum, glaring at me in brazen innocence. "What?"

"If this goes missing, Tye," Klarissa says, her eyes narrowing, "I'll make Coal's adventures at the whipping post yesterday seem like a pleasant pastime."

The corners of Tye's mouth twitch.

"Please, sit," Klarissa says, gesturing amiably with both hands and waiting for us to obey. "As I was saying"—she clears her throat in an attempt to reclaim her earlier momentum—"the council regrets any inconvenience that the glitch in the wards may have caused. I assure you, the matter will be investigated fully."

Heat rises to my face, my fists clenching in my silk-covered lap. Klarissa has already tried to have me killed once, and she was certainly the damn culprit behind the failed ward. The males might be content to let this pass, but exhausted and furious as I still am, I'm ready to state the truth aloud. Before I can, however, Tye's arms encircle me, pulling me back against his muscled body—and halfway onto his chair. His scent, with which I was very intimately acquainted an hour ago, heats my skin, but my eyes narrow on Klarissa nonetheless. I open my mouth to—

I gasp, feeling Tye lick my ear.

Stars.

"If you could do us all the courtesy of keeping your breeches on for a few more minutes, I would appreciate it," Klarissa finally snaps, her silk voice crackling through the air. Drawing a deep breath, she regains her composure and turns pointedly toward River, who waits in pious attentiveness. "I came to offer my congratulations on your quint's successful completion of a trial, River," Klarissa says, her voice admirably formal. "I must also mention that, had you told the council you've a weaver in your midst, we could have done a great deal to assist. Your secret helped no one, prince of Slait. We are on the same side—the one fighting against Mors."

River's face is stone, but my eyes widen and even the feel of Tye's arms around me is not enough to halt my sharply indrawn breath.

Klarissa turns toward me, lifting a manicured brow. "The Elders Council is not a decoration, Leralynn. We work with facts, history, research, and observation at least half as well as the princess of Slait does." Giving Autumn a small bow, Klarissa strides around the table, her delicate hand brushing across River's broad shoulders before settling on the nape of Shade's neck.

Shade stiffens, his eyes dull and filled with pain. His nostrils flare but he stays still beneath the female's touch. My chest tightens. Shade has spoken to me as little as Coal has, though Shade's distance feels different. Quiet. Fearful. Like an animal hiding a wound that it fears will mark it as prey. I little understand, little care *why* he won't let me near him. But there is no choice about permitting Klarissa's touch, it seems.

A moment later, magic, shimmering like liquid silver, suddenly spreads from Klarissa's hand to cover Shade's neck, back, and shoulders. The male arches, tense and silent, the agony flashing through his eyes setting my soul aflame.

I jerk in Tye's hold.

"Steady, lass," Tye whispers in my ear. "That's healing magic. And Klarissa's affinity for it is the strongest known."

Healing. I almost laugh at the absurd irony, but even that bitter humor fades as Klarissa pulls away her hand.

Shade turns toward her. I watch for the furious indignation I expect to see flashing in those golden eyes, but instead find a mix of question and plea.

My chest squeezes. So there *is* a wound. A real one. One bad enough that Shade is too frightened to admit its extent. Beneath the table, I extend my leg slowly and press my calf against his.

A moment later, Shade presses back, his attention on Klarissa's inevitable diagnosis.

She pats his trembling shoulder. "There is a great deal more damage than I can correct in the middle of a dining hall, shifter, but . . . I'm confident you will regain your magic. For now, transition down to your wolf. It is safer for you and will aid in the healing."

I startle, my eyes widening. "*Regain* his magic? Is it—"

The pressure of Shade's leg on mine intensifies, leaning into me.

Klarissa clicks her tongue, meeting my gaze. "It's gone, yes. Your friend is fortunate that Coal there pulled him back as quickly as he did, or the wards would have burned him out completely." She shifts her attention back to her patient, her tone hardening. "There is no healing death, Shade. You are smart enough to know that. What in the name of Lunos were you thinking?"

The question hangs in the air, Shade's eyes unwilling to meet mine.

Klarissa sighs and studies her nails, which are manicured with a pearly black paint that plays off her dress. "Unless, of course, you weren't thinking, were letting that mating instinct wreak havoc on you instead. There are ways to ease that transition too, you know. Exercises, warded charms, herbs. If you wish for help, all you need to do is ask." Without waiting for an answer, Klarissa walks away, leaving crackling silence in her wake.

Coal's lips pull back into a snarl. "That vicious bi—"

"I would urge you to consider your next words carefully," Elder Elidyr says in a too-calm voice that has

Coal shutting his mouth at once. Elidyr nods and shifts his gaze until it rests on River's. Though not as large as River, the elder has the same calm presence that I remember from the council chamber. "Klarissa is not incorrect, you know. Now that the trials have revealed Leralynn's nature, we can help you train. Help you become the quint that the magic has chosen you to be."

Trust the council. Even coming from Elidyr, the words sound ludicrous.

"If I discover a shred of proof that Klarissa was behind the ward's failure," River says, his words black ice. "I will bring down the Citadel around her ears. Please make no mistake about it, Elder."

"How . . . brazen." Elidyr's oval face straightens as he hooks his thumbs into the belt of his riding leathers. "While you are chasing that fiction, River, you might also examine what Klarissa has been doing to protect Lunos from Mors in the past decade, while your quint was dormant. Please, enjoy the rest of your dinner and try to decide whether it's Klarissa or Mors's Emperor Jawrar whom you five intend to spend your destiny fighting."

<<THE END of *Mistake of Magic*. Lera's adventure continues in *Trial of Three*, Power of Five Book 3.>>

New Adult Fantasy Romance

POWER OF FIVE (Reverse Harem Fantasy)

POWER OF FIVE

MISTAKE OF MAGIC

TRIAL OF THREE

Young Adult Fantasy Novels

TIDES

FIRST COMMAND (Prequel Novella)

AIR AND ASH

WAR AND WIND

SEA AND SAND

SCOUT

TRACING SHADOWS

UNRAVELING DARKNESS

TILDOR

THE CADET OF TILDOR

~

SIGN UP FOR NEW RELEASE NOTIFICATIONS at
www.subscribepage.com/TIDES

ABOUT THE AUTHOR

Alex Lidell is the Amazon Breakout Novel Awards finalist author of THE CADET OF TILDOR (Penguin, 2013) and Amazon Top 100 Kindle Bestseller POWER OF FIVE (Danger Bearing Press, 2018). She is an avid horseback rider, a (bad) hockey player, and an ice-cream addict. Born in Russia, Alex learned English in elementary school, where a thoughtful librarian placed a copy of Tamora Pierce's ALANNA in Alex's hands. In addition to becoming the first English book Alex read for fun, ALANNA started Alex's life long love for fantasy books. Alex lives in Washington, DC. Join Alex's newsletter for news, bonus content and sneak peeks: www.subscribepage.com/TIDES Find out more on Alex's website: www.alexlidell.com

SIGN UP FOR NEWS AND RELEASE NOTIFICATIONS

Connect with Alex!
www.alexlidell.com
alex@alexlidell.com

CPSIA information can be obtained
at www.ICGtesting.com
Printed in the USA
BVHW081124160921
616890BV00001B/32

9 781949 347012